Drought

CW01501986

'Where's your father?' the psychic asks, in London. She's wearing a thin chenille jumper over her large pointy breasts. 'I can see your grandfather, but not your father: are you here to tell me what happened to you?'

I nod. I shake my head. I nod again. The psychic asks me about my life, following the question with a string of expletives and smiles, while I am shaking, holding a twelve-kilogram pink quartz stone in my hands.

I have ended up here on the advice of my new boyfriend, who thinks the psychic is great fun, and that she could perhaps help me. I also think she's fun, but I'm distracted by the fact that she is way more attractive than I expected. All this pink isn't helping either. I tell her I feel like I will never write again, and that, since the Disaster, even falling in love has become frightening. I'm not even sure if the plants on my terrace will make it through next winter. Nor us, with them.

'It's just fear,' she says. 'The short answer would be yes. Yes, to everything.'

'Are you sure?'

'This is the first and the last time you're allowed to ask me if I'm sure about something.'

I shut up, stroking the pink quartz as if it were a cat.

'What's going on, then?' the psychic asks.

'The rock isn't purring,' I say. She smiles. She has a gold tooth, or maybe I do.

'Are you ready?' she insists. Her nipples nod along to the same question. 'Shall we go back?' I nod once, then again, towards the whole universe. I shut my eyes and I try to go back. To pick an important day. A recent, important day in my life, in which a cerebral aneurysm, the end of my greatest love story and a horrific head-on collision will forever coexist. When I choose to face the Disaster, I immediately lose myself. I can no longer feel the weight of the pink quartz in my hands, and the house I am in no longer has walls. There is only light, heat and desert.

On the day that I would later call the Day of the Disaster, the city was steaming.

At 2 p.m., when the temperature had become unbearable, I went to my mother's gallery. The gallery is on the outskirts of Milan, near the motorway, in an impoverished, borderland neighbourhood. Once upon a time, my grandfather's printing press occupied the same premises.

Under the sun and alone in the universe, I was reading the graffiti on the walls and counting the cigarette butts at my feet, to avoid going in. There was drought in everything

We Will Be Forest

'A highly original and compelling account of starting over that both touched and amused me by turns. Ilaria's distinctive voice lights the page and the ending will resonate long after you finish reading.' – Rebecca Frayn, *Lost in Ibiza*

'The title is wonderful and so is the content. Ilaria Bernardini has a way of talking about caring for plants as if she were discussing how to cherish your love for someone, and vice versa.' – Serena Dandini, *Io Donna - Corriere della Sera*

'The most lifelike literary product to have appeared in Italy in years. Painful, moving, beautiful.' – Teresa Ciabatti, *Corriere della Sera*

'You laugh in a slightly bitter and slightly sweet way, which is truly moving.' – Annalena Benini, *il Foglio*

'A forest that grows under an incessant gentle rainfall of words which Ilaria sows skilfully, making it immense, full and green.' – Federica Bosco, *Tuttolibri, La Stampa*

'Through a powerful botanical metaphor and the happy device of burying the void by "creating a forest", Ilaria Bernardini fashions a story which is also a hymn to life.' – Ilaria Zaffino, *Robinson*

'Its most striking feature is a willingness to use the narrative medium to tell the whole truth about oneself.' – Valentina della Seta, *Il Venerdì di Repubblica*

'A deeply intimate, enchanted novel.' – Marta Cervino, *Marie Claire*

'A manual on how not to be afraid.' – Victoria Cabello, *GRAZIA*

WE
WILL
BE
FOREST

ILARIA BERNARDINI

First published in 2024
in partnership with Whitefox Publishing

www.wearewhitefox.com

ISBN 9781916797147
Also available as an eBook
ISBN 9781916797154

Translated by Livia Franchini
Cover artwork by Flaminia Veronesi
Designed and typeset by Anna Green
Cover design by Emma Ewbank
Project management by Whitefox
Printed and bound by CPI Group (UK) Ltd, Croydon CR0 4YY

Contents

This is a true story,
in so far as I remember it.

that had ever existed, even in my mouth, and even in my heart. The times when my grandfather had taken me to visit his factory, on the other hand, had been prosperous ones, full of dew and blossoming plants, and he had given me freshly printed books to take home as a gift. The Roland Ultra, a machine which seemed to me enormous, elephant-like, spat them out. I hadn't opened those books since and didn't know where they had ended up. Under that sky, and in front of that factory, I wanted them all back for myself and for my son, Nico. I needed the books to remind myself of how easy those times had been, when all we'd had to do was open our arms, raising our palms up to the sky. Sticking our tongue out was all that it took and rain would have inevitably fallen, to satiate our thirst. I wanted the books back, mostly to cry over them for the very same reasons, and in order to dilute my pain with the memory of how deeply our grandfather had loved us. I wanted to forget that I had given up on so many things, and believe that I'd been able to look after my family and our stuff with an appropriate level of care. But I knew I had lost so many books and pens and lovers, and way too much time. If only I could touch those covers again, crack open those pages, I was sure that my grandfather's books would have made everything come back.

When my mobile rang, I checked it wasn't a number to do with my son; when I saw that it wasn't, I didn't pick up. I stuffed the phone in my bag, but it began ringing again. I pressed mute without checking twice. Nico at the time was four years old. He was a sweet, kind child, very thin, who looked a little bit like I'd always imagined Pinocchio as a real boy: clever, cute and a little melancholic. I had to keep an eye out for Lucignolo, the fox and the cat, and all the candy that villains handed out at funfairs. I took turns playing Geppetto or the Fairy with Turquoise Hair, depending on whether that day I felt like a moustachioed old lady or beautiful and full of magic.

'Can you hear my voice?' shouts the psychic in London. I nod, yes. Or maybe I don't, because she throws in a couple more swear words. I nod with more vehemence. 'Tell me your story,' she repeats. 'Write for me!'

I took an epic step, as if to jump to the moon, to enter the courtyard of the gallery, and inside was my present, and inside was my past. I spotted Maria, my mother's assistant. Maria was also a friend of my sister Diana, so I had known her forever. When she smiled, I decided I could stay. And anyway, I had no other choice: I'd been found out now, there were witnesses. I said hello to Maria, kissed her on the cheeks and we exchanged a few words. I had similar relationships with most of my two sisters' and my brother's friends. A few words, a quick update, two pecks on the cheeks. Maria's face looked wretched, but I paid no attention to it. My brain simply stored the information, without processing it, until a long time later, when everything would begin to feel meaningful around me, each sagging eye bag, every single drop of sweat telling the story of the end of the world as we knew it.

I went up to my mother's office and we talked about my life: I was about to break up with my husband and move house, and we still hadn't told Nico what was happening.

My mother stared at me and said something about my proclivity for never being satisfied. She added something else about the poor boy. That's what she called him, *that poor boy*. And I saw Nico as a poor boy with scraped knees and skinny arms. My mother was sixty-two; me, thirty-four.

'You look grumpy,' says the psychic in London.

'I'm putting on my mother's face when she's being strict,' I confirm.

My mother had had four children and she had worked as a publisher and a journalist. She'd dropped it all to look after my grandfather's business when he'd passed away. She hadn't enjoyed it. It had been a difficult and lonely endeavour, which had disrupted the rest of her dreams. She'd done it because she was an only child, because my grandmother had never worked a day in her life and the situation my grandfather had left behind was complicated. Meanwhile, she'd managed to build herself an art gallery on the former premises of the printing press. But even that had proved lonely and exhausting. The building was in ruins, a health and safety hazard with no heating system. The city was immobile. There was no money to fix the gallery and now my mother had convinced herself that its future lay in turning it into a ping-pong venue for teenagers. She wanted to call it Pong.

On the wall behind my mother, my grandfather's photograph and several other pictures and paintings were all staring at me. In a black-and-white print a woman, the artist, with her back to the viewer, spread her arms out wide, wax candles melting on her shoulders.

'What's the name of that artist?' I asked my mother and all the ghosts in the room. My mother remained silent. She didn't seem to remember the artist's name, though I was sure she must know it well. I wondered, if both of us stayed silent forever, would the candles burn to the quick? Would the flames trickle down to burn the artist's skin, then the print and, finally, the whole room with us in it? Suddenly, my mother remembered the name and she nearly screamed it. I nodded. I had known it too, and I, too, had forgotten it. The candles kept burning, their flames straining towards the ceiling. I wanted to blow on them.

'If I end up forgetting everything, leave me walking on a beach,' my mother said. She always said that, and she'd always been convinced that one day she would lose her wits and forget everything about life. She'd probably even forget this conversation, and so eventually it wouldn't have mattered whether I left her walking on a beach or on whatever road near her house.

That room made me want to steal. Case in point: a black-and-white triptych in the boardroom. It represented three islands pictured from afar, which disappeared and re-appeared once again. My mother's house also made me want to steal: her cups, lamps, smoother bedsheets. Her pens, which wrote better than mine, and our photographs as children. Now we were no longer children, we constantly had to remind ourselves of that fact. We had our own houses, our own children. My older sister Allegra had been living abroad for twenty years, first in France, then in Cambodia. For the last thirteen years she'd been in New Zealand. Teo, Diana and even I had all come back to Milan a few years back.

'You're spoilt. It's probably my fault in the way I raised you kids,' my mother said.

'We've stopped loving each other,' I said.

'You always want more.'

'Do others always want less?' Whenever she used the word 'kids', I became a kid again.

'You know what I mean.'

'Give me a practical example of someone who always wants less.' We were quiet for a bit. Me, a kid, and her, a kid's mother. 'Can I have the photograph with the islands?' I asked. 'We just don't want to be together anymore; it's nobody's fault,' I added. My heart shrank in my chest. All the living animals on planet Earth – and I with them, and my mother with them – no longer had anything to drink.

I went out to the courtyard. I looked for water without finding it. I could have been a stronger person in my love story. I could have held in there. In a few years, perhaps, everything would have fallen back into place and all this grief would have taken on a universal meaning, greater than my own sadness today and greater than all of us altogether. If I'd held on, my eventual victory would have far exceeded my pain.

I sat down on a short wooden bench. Maria sat next to me. We had known each other for years, perhaps forever, but though I knew her face, and a few random facts about her life, Maria was otherwise a stranger to me. She wore her hair long, down to her bottom, a shortsleeved T-shirt and boyish slacks, and had the general air of someone who didn't care too much about clothes. She'd been the same as a child. As a child, I later discovered, Maria had also liked frogspawn, worms and other animals. She used to record the characteristics of living creatures on index cards. She'd filled in a file for the Shar Pei breed of dog, of which she'd been very proud. Maria was always drawing. With her pen, she organised, studied and rearranged planet Earth.

That afternoon, Maria hadn't been sure whether she wanted to come to the gallery. She'd recently started to volunteer at an allotment, and that morning she hadn't felt well. Possibly heatstroke. She'd been unable to plant three seedlings in a row, and she'd become restless. She had a headache. One of the reasons Maria worked at the allotment was to study the reproductive processes of vegetables, and over forty varieties of tomatoes grew in the greenhouses there.

'I went to art college, I work with art, and artists, and I can't even plant a row of three zinnia,' she'd thought that morning.

In school, she'd been a head-girl type: good in all subjects, always top marks, always precise to the point of fastidiousness. But the heat beat down on the allotment and Maria had had to wet her head. When the pain hadn't subsided, she'd lain down on a brick wall and listened to a bunch of old women chat. She didn't like those women. She'd wished they'd be quiet.

'They were saying a bunch of stupid, racist things,' she explained to me, when we talked about it, months later.

She'd breathed deeply and waited another ten minutes or so. She'd thought, if I feel better, I'll go back to the gallery; if not, so be it. When she'd felt better, she'd travelled across the city.

The main reason Maria had wanted to make it to my mother's gallery was that she knew Alessandro, Diana's boyfriend, had had a motorbike accident in the night. The Day of the Disaster had in fact already begun before dawn, with a head-on collision. Maria was frightened and wanted to know if my mother had more information about it. We all knew that Alessandro was fighting between life and death. Before she got to the gallery, before she bumped into me and spoke to me, Maria had phoned her own mother. She'd said, I'm done living precariously.

'Everything disappears so quickly,' she'd whispered.

'You've just got to live,' her mother had said.

So Maria had come into the gallery, and I arrived a few minutes later.

'And you chose to begin by telling me about a printing machine and a set of photographs you wanted to steal, before you thought to mention the motorbike accident?' the psychic says.

'Have I been talking?' I say. My lips are sealed. If I have, I haven't been using my voice.

'You've just asked me, "Have I been talking?", so I'm pretty sure you're talking, babe,' the psychic says. She puts her hand on mine. Back of my hand, palm of hers. She shows me how to stroke the quartz. I follow her movement. It's continuous, slow. Suddenly, she rubs the rock quickly, with vigour.

'Clean, Anna! Clean!' she says. So I start to clean.

On the bench Maria and I talked about Alessandro. Diana and Alessandro had been together for four years. In fact, he and my sister had just broken up again, and she had left two days earlier, her destination Berlin. They'd broken up before and it wasn't clear if this was a definitive thing. Sometimes, as soon as they'd broken up, they planned a trip to the Philippines. Or they broke up, kissed other people, then fell out because they'd kissed other people, and circled back eventually to talking about a discovery trip to the Philippines. Diana didn't want to have children for a while; she wasn't sure about anything except for the fact she and Alessandro had a mutual interest in the Philippines. So she'd gone to Berlin.

Alessandro, on the other hand, had stayed behind in the city. The previous evening, he'd gone out to a bar, and when the bar had shut, he'd got back on his motorbike. It was 3 a.m., and, as he rounded a bend too quickly, he ran into a pothole. The bike had slid out from under him. His helmet had come off as he'd slipped. He'd flown up in the air and then crashed back down to the ground. This, at least, was what I knew then: that Alessandro was in hospital, in a medically induced coma, his life at risk. They were operating on his aorta.

'I'm scared,' I say to the psychic. I steady my hand. I don't want to be cleaning anything. I don't want to be here, wiping a rock. I have no time for such idiocy, nor psychics.

'Smile,' she says. 'Smile, even if you're faking it; smile even if you can't do it properly.' So I smile, faking it. Not properly. She hugs me, or maybe she's tackling me so I can't run away. She smells like Marseille soap, curry and moisturiser. I can't breathe.

'Hold me properly,' she says. I hold her properly. 'Hold me better. Breathe against my belly.' I try to breathe against her belly. I try to relax. To hold her better.

'OK, good. And now go back for real,' she shouts in my ear. 'Stop pretending. Trust me, for fuck's sake!'

Night Everywhere

While I was at my mother's gallery, talking to Maria about Alessandro on that first day, while his life was about to end, while we kept saying the word 'death', over and over again, everything seemed like sand, a desert: there were no roots, no meaning.

'We won't be saved!' I wanted to scream. 'I don't ever want to die,' I would have insisted, if it could have saved me.

Everything was about to collapse; the question was when and how. Even the city had never looked so ugly. And the factory, and the summer. Us and our lives. The end of our loves. The financial crisis; the jellyfish invading our seas, making it impossible for us to dive. Italy, finally drowning and dying in among its ruins. Alessandro's chemical coma and our melancholy. Writing, getting one's voice out there, in the loudest silence. Living; loving. Drinking water.

Meanwhile, Diana was on her way back from Berlin. The previous evening, she'd deliberately ignored two calls from

Alessandro's mother. On the third attempt, she'd plucked up the courage to answer, and received news of the accident. She'd sent a postcard to my son from the airport – something she always did, and didn't forego even on a day like that – and, right after, she'd jumped on a plane.

That's what Maria and I were discussing while the world was collapsing in on itself.

'I'm not feeling well,' Maria said at one point, while we sat in that courtyard, in the Palaeocene, having bid our goodbye to the last of the giant reptiles. She looked pale and frightened. We were still sitting on the small bench, and around us still stood my grandfather's factory. The world was still the world as we knew it, in so far as fibre cement and concrete were concerned.

'I'm not the kind of person who's over the top about this kind of thing,' Maria said.

'What kind of things do you mean?'

'I mean, I'm really unwell,' she whispered.

My heartbeat changed. Maybe it was the heat. Or that infinite sadness, or Maria's skin that had turned grey, as if to ask me once more whether we would survive until summer's end. Survive what? I couldn't tell. It wasn't just the accident, and the pain, but something larger, beyond what we were able to comprehend. Surviving life itself. Like a dog, I could sense its sickness, and our own. This wasn't panic, it was all true: a meteor was about to fall on our planet and extinguish us too. My body was ringing with alarm for the impending disaster.

Later, Maria told me she'd known she was dying. This is it,

dying, she'd thought with some clarity, but she hadn't said it because it was such an impossible thought to handle. So, instead of saying I'm dying, she said, 'May I have some water?'

'My head is about to explode,' she added.

'Shall I get you some water?' I asked. Shall I hold your head, so it doesn't explode? I thought. Does water still exist on this planet?

'Call an ambulance first.'

I took out my phone. Meanwhile, my mother had walked out into the courtyard, just as Maria started to vomit. My mother came closer, to see what was going on.

'I'm cold,' Maria said. She was sweating. Her long hair was wet, plastered to her neck. Her skin was a colour that didn't exist in nature, or life. My mother pulled up Maria's hair. She ran a wet cloth over Maria's shoulders and face. Maria threw up again. She was frail, lost. We gave her a bin for the vomit.

'I can't move my neck,' she hissed.

My mother later said that the main thing she remembered was the trembling of Maria's lips. I remember how the light had suddenly changed. It was night everywhere and we couldn't understand a single thing – words, the order of sentences. I remember thinking, here's how a waste-paper bin turns into a vomit bin, just like the chair you usually sit in eventually turns into the chair you sat in to die, a factory into a desert: a matter of objects changing the function they perform in a story. If someone had asked me, is that the sun up there in the sky? I would have certainly replied no, it isn't.

'And what about you?' the psychic asks. 'Are you there?'

'Can you see me?' I try.

'It doesn't matter, you must exist nonetheless,' she laughs.

I called an ambulance and I tried to explain to the operator what was happening. I said that Maria's eyes had turned white. She was throwing up. She had a terrible headache.

'She's twenty-nine,' I added.

They didn't seem convinced it was an emergency at first, and I'm not sure what it was I said that made them change their mind. Maybe it helped that I was screaming. Maybe it didn't. The receptionist didn't ask whether the sun was still up in the sky. Whether we were all afraid of death on that day too. I didn't ask her how she carried on breathing every day, in the middle of all this fear. I didn't ask for her name, and that's why I don't know it today. If I had asked for her name, now I could write her into my story.

'It might just be a severe migraine,' the nameless, story-less operator suggested.

'But she can't move her neck,' I screamed. 'It's terrifying not to be able to move your neck!'

The ambulance took fifteen minutes to arrive. In those fifteen minutes I understood that there is a great difference between our emotional experience of time and the measurable units we use to keep track of it. Between being afraid of not moving one's neck, and an actual inability to move it. Meanwhile, Maria kept throwing up, while my mother tended to her, though it was clear to all three of us that there wasn't much we could do to help. We'd never seen anything like it. Not even my mother, who'd had four children, more friends and more years behind her, and had witnessed more pain and more illness than either of us – not even she had seen anything like it. Still, she tried to soothe us, like mothers do, like she's especially good at doing.

'Maybe it's a digestive problem,' my mother said.

She tried to talk about normal things, to distract Maria, to make things easy again. It's so hot today! We always make the mistake of drinking ice-cold water too quickly. She also suffered from sudden migraines – could something similar be happening? I listened to my mother and held on to the hope she was offering, though I knew perfectly well that my mother had never suffered from sudden migraines.

'Or, it could be heatstroke,' my mother suggested.

If it wasn't an excess of cold, it could be an excess of heat, couldn't it? My mother listed various other possibilities, insisting it couldn't be anything serious. We believed her, with some part of ourselves, as a part of ourselves always believes in mothers, especially when we are sick, and need care. We don't need to believe our mothers when it comes to love, or duty, but we do if it's about fear or illness – fear of the darkness, or physical pain.

By that point, Maria could barely speak. I'd brought a large, thin scarf with me, to protect myself from the chill of the air conditioning. Maria was shaking, so we wrapped her in it. It was at least thirty-five degrees in our desert. Thirty-five million, maybe.

'I'll check if they're coming,' I said.

I went to the gate, and while I waited for the ambulance, I called my husband and explained what was happening. I said I was afraid. He'd been on the receiving end of all my fears for so many years, and I of his. Who would be there to console me tomorrow? Who would I be writing my stories for? Was Maria dying?

When the paramedics arrived, they took Maria's blood pressure. They lay her down on a stretcher and asked her if she could remember her name, when and where she was born. Maria remembered everything. She remembered that people are born, and specifically when and where it had happened to her.

'My head's exploding,' she said again. Her voice was weaker and weaker.

'Have you been travelling abroad?' the older paramedic asked.

'No,' she whispered.

'Maria has been working on an allotment,' we explained.

The paramedics nodded, as if they'd understood something. Understood what? I wondered. Who was Maria? Did working in an allotment make you sick? The younger paramedics put white masks on and asked us to step away.

'It could be meningitis,' they said.

Another thing my mother remembers from that day are the droplets of water that formed around Maria's lips, the only water in the middle of the drought.

'There were so many – a weird shape.'

'Like hearts?' I asked. 'Stars?'

'Don't be silly.'

'What else do you remember?'

'That you immediately thought it was something deadly, due to your penchant for fear and emergency. You're always afraid of everything.'

'You too,' I said. 'But you like pretending you aren't.'

When the paramedics said 'meningitis' I stepped back and, as I did so, I felt guilty. My first thought was my son, the second was me. I could no longer see Maria's pain. I could no longer hear her crying. I was only thinking of my family.

Was this the end I'd always imagined would hit us too early? What was the point of breaking up with my husband, if we were all going to die anyway? Or conversely, why was I even worried about leaving him – I could do anything, even be alone, starting this second. We were all going to die anyway.

Maria was put on a stretcher and carried into the ambulance, and my mother told her she'd follow all the way to the hospital. She didn't hesitate for one moment to go with Maria, because mothers never get sick and never get tired. That's what I thought mothers were like before I'd become one myself. Whereas I found I was always tired, and I got sick practically every time Nico was sick. I'd also found out my mother was tired – often more tired than me.

'Both hospitals are on the same side of the city. They'll let us know our exact destination soon,' a paramedic said.

My mother took her car keys, grabbed Maria's bag and asked me to shut the gate after I left.

'I'll call your parents,' I said to Maria. But she was no longer able to speak.

Alone in the courtyard, I called Maria's mother and told her, 'Maria's not well; she's going to hospital.' What would I do, I wondered, if a similar call reached me about Nico? I heard my own scream in that alternative version of the story, in a possible future where that really happened.

'Which hospital?' Maria's mother asked.

'They're just deciding. You can call my mother in five.' Left or right? Meningitis or heatstroke? Life or death?

'She was so tired and upset about Alessandro,' Maria's mother explained.

'Don't worry,' I said, and a shiver ran down my spine.

I hung up and after the shivers, tears finally came. Had I gone into too much detail, telling Maria about Alessandro? Had I used too many adjectives, put too much emphasis on his injuries? Was I too direct? Did I unsettle her and upset her further with my words? Back then, I was always thinking: is it my fault? In those days the question seemed to apply both to Maria and my marriage. My narcissist delirium meant that I was such an excellent storyteller I was able to make someone else's head explode on the spot. That night I fell asleep feeling dirty. Nico was sleeping in the other room, my husband on the living room sofa. The heat was relentless and everything was relentless. For two or three nights in a row, I swallowed a quarter of a sleeping pill and said my prayers backwards, from the end to the beginning, from the end of the night to the beginning of the day, hoping to sleep, to change the direction of time, to get back to the moment just before dawn, just before the Big Bang.

The Ruins

In the other hospital, Alessandro wasn't getting better. His chemically induced coma continued. They'd stuck a tube in his groin, reaching his aorta at shoulder-level, and fixed a tear there with a tiny, netted balloon.

'Everything's working great for the time being,' the doctors said. 'We just don't know exactly how it'll work in twenty or thirty years. We've no reference framework to go by yet.'

Likewise, it was Alessandro's first passage on Earth, and so the truth was that we can never truly predict the future in any specific instance, nor for any specific person we meet. There was no other Alessandro as a reference case to go by, and there never would be. After his operation, they gave Alessandro a piece of paper to carry with him at all times, for the rest of his life. It said, in medical terms: everything's working great for the time being. Heart. Aorta. Your life. Your death. For now. Afterwards, we'll have to see how things go, the paper said.

Following rupture of the aortic isthmus in context of a polytraumatic event, Mr Alessandro Parrella underwent endovascular stent-grafting of the descending thoracic aortic; extension of periaortic haematoma required covering of the left subclavian orifice. At discharge, the prosthesis is intact and stable in its correct position, of no clinical concern; the upper left arm is sufficiently assisted by the collateral vessels and does not present signs of weakness or heightened sensitivity. No clinical follow-up protocol exists as of yet for this procedure; we recommend yearly thoracic spine X-ray, inclusive of obliques, to confirm the structural integrity of the endoprosthesis, since repeated exposure to angio-CT in such a young patient may lead to excessive exposure. Further investigation may be reserved in the instance of legitimate clinical concern.

The following day, it looked like Alessandro had escaped the worst. So they got to work on his broken wrist. The day after that, the news was bad again: Alessandro had got pneumonia, and antibiotics were not working. I pictured Alessandro with pneumonia, like a sick person in a movie, grey skin, dry lips, eyes squeezed tight. In my head, Alessandro was wearing an oxygen mask, and Heidi the milkmaid and Heidi's grandfather sat by his bedside, hoping for better news in the morning, just as it had been better news for Peter, the goatherd boy, every time he'd crashed his sled in the Swiss mountains. Nico and I had been reading about Heidi and Peter's story – they, too, knew quite a lot about illness.

Unlike Peter, Alessandro had spoken to his father, moments before he'd been put to sleep. 'I'm sorry I'm dying,' he'd told him. Months later, talking to me about it, that sentence came back to his mind, and Alessandro began to cry. I did too.

'That night, I had a real 1950s dream – everything was purple, ochre yellow and red,' he said. He enjoyed the cocktail of drugs he was given during his coma; it had made him feel good. He said it had been an arousing dream, full of beautiful, sexy, dark-skinned women who danced for him.

If I had a billion to bet, like in a cartoon, and I could sneak into Alessandro's dream, I'm sure I'd find the psychic there, in her pink chenille, with her pointy breasts and that huge confidence of hers. All of it for him. She'd probably wink. She'd tell me, don't look at me, look at your life. Write! Love!

After that first, hot night, I called my mother to ask about Maria. It wasn't meningitis. She'd had a brain aneurysm and had been operated on urgently. Now she was in intensive care; they were keeping her under, tubes coming out of her head. Her long hair had been shaved off. The desert and the drought had even taken over her head. They'd found another aneurysm that could burst at any time. Maria's parents were very worried, Maria herself was terrified. She'd been put to sleep and operated on again. After the second operation, Maria was no longer kept in her own private room, and was moved to a communal ward where her boyfriend was finally allowed to visit. He brought her food and, for a very long time afterwards, he'd continue to massage her legs with essential oils. They were in love. They had a home together, a lot of plants, two bicycles and one bed.

When she came out of her own chemical coma, in intensive care, Maria's vision was foggy, and she couldn't recognise anyone. She didn't realise she hadn't got her glasses on, and she thought, if she lived, she would always see the world like this, out of focus, blurry.

'A nurse was helping me,' Maria would later tell me. 'He was a very large man. He busied himself around me and cared for me. It was like seeing an enormous stain. I really loved that stain.'

It was summer and there was less work to do, so meeting up at Alessandro's bedside became a habit. In the hospital corridors, we discussed him and much else. My mother would later tell me that she'd resented the social aspect of Alessandro's operations, how everybody had wanted to share in the drama. Later still, she'd take it back. What was wrong with wanting to be together? What was wrong with other people's love – even mine – ending, if hers had also ended? Though of course hers hadn't really ended in the same way.

'How's Alessandro doing?' she'd ask when we arrived at the hospital.

'They came out two hours ago to tell us he's doing well, isn't doing well, the operation is underway, the operation is about to begin.' And so on and so forth. It seems strange to say 'and so on and so forth' about such a matter, but there were so many operations, and so many updates, that it really was and so on and so forth, or it felt that way.

Whenever I looked at Alessandro's mum, I cried. She smoked incessantly and was a rock. We had beers together outside the hospital, and sometimes, after we'd cried, we'd laugh.

My husband and I were about to leave town for several weeks and wanted to say goodbye to Alessandro. We were still trying to do things together, to follow the plan we had already organised. On the one hand, we were hoping things could go back to the way they were; on the other, we were certain that it could never happen. Everything was blurry and we, too, loved a stain. Out of focus, we were still us: we still had plans together and we had plans for our son.

We drove the loaded car to the hospital and parked by the gardens. On the lawn, we saw some friends who had spent the morning outside the operating theatre, and waved at them from afar, smiling. My feeling that life was entirely falling apart became clearer and clearer. Even the construction sites around the city seemed to have sprung up to remind me of the holes beneath them. I couldn't take a step without thinking of falling. Falling, lying down, never getting up again. Walking on ruins was difficult, and a torture in thirty-five million degrees. So long as Nico keeps standing, I kept telling myself, it will be OK, because falling into a hole, for him, was a much greater danger.

In his room, Alessandro, who had actually fallen, was the picture of effort and resistance. I cried. But he and I also laughed, and we talked about the new wing of the hospital, which was such a pleasing building.

'It looks like a Japanese hotel,' we said.

None of us had ever been to Japan. My husband and I would never go to Japan together. Japan is far, but not that far. Maybe there was somebody I'd fall madly in love with, in Japan. Et cetera.

Alessandro was in and out of the operating theatre like he didn't care, or so he said. I wondered which of the blows that had altered his facial features was destined to stay. I thought about his heart. His fear, and ours. I asked myself, will Alessandro be alive in two months? Will Maria? Will we? If all of us will be alive in two months, who'll be the first to die next? Alessandro had two metal bars screwed into his hips, which stuck out of the covers, red with disinfectant.

'We have to leave,' I said to Alessandro, and, in a way, I was saying the same to my husband.

'Have a good trip,' we all said, and each of us attached our own meaning to the sentence.

Over the summer, Maria and Alessandro spoke to each other from their respective hospital beds. In a way, the scene was intrinsically comic. My sister stayed by Alessandro's side, and they no longer talked about breaking up. Or else, they'd come to a tacit agreement: they wanted to be by each other's side, so they stuck by each other's side as they discussed once again that fateful trip to the Philippines. We all got distracted, and distraction was always a guilty state, because even distracted, I was sharply aware of my own lack of care towards my two friends. We hadn't been the closest of friends; Alessandro and Maria hadn't been people I'd regularly spoken to, but how was it right to be well while they were suffering? Maria had fallen ill right in front of my eyes and was still in a very serious condition.

Alessandro had spent Christmases and birthdays at our house, and he was now risking his life with metal screws in his body. From the news we received, sometimes it looked like one was worse than the other, sometimes the reverse.

'I felt guilty that Maria was suffering, physically, more than I was. I was drunk; it was my fault,' Alessandro would tell me later.

Guilt, in other words, kept assailing us all. After the first few weeks, I stopped calling on Alessandro in hospital, and I no longer contacted his or Maria's parents to keep track of the news. I knew I should have, but I didn't. I listened to the news we received and worried about them. I listened to more news and felt better. I understood little things, such as the fact that there's never a typical recovery and that precise diagnoses do not exist. That one in two people has an aneurysm ready to burst in their head. I learnt more about myself and felt sorry about my weaknesses and the distance I put between me and others. I was consumed by my own life and the end of my love. How to get to the end of each day, how to write again, how to look after my baby. So, the weeks passed, and then summer ended. We went back to the city; we signed Nico up to a new school and I began looking for a new flat.

'You're tired of writing as homework,' says the psychic in London.

There is a growing smell of curry. Fresh ginger.

'Don't you want to try and love again? Write again? Otherwise, you'll be doomed to come back to this Earth another billion times,' the psychic insists. She chews gum and moulds a large ball with it, which is a planet: I can see the sea, the land, the birds and the fish. She whispers something I don't understand, and the smell of incense suffocates me, and it is good to suffocate, like a chemically induced sleep.

'Was it you dancing in Alessandro's dream while he was in a coma?' I ask her.

'If you keep getting distracted and never committing to your own narrative, we might as well end it here and have some dinner. I'm a really great cook and I'm very hungry,' the psychic says. 'What do you feel like? Chicken? Fish?'

'Sorry,' I whisper. 'Anyway, I'm vegetarian.'

'Vegetarian. That's funny! Listen, babe, you don't know if you want to write and how, you don't know whether to love or how. Why don't you just love, and write, and shut up about it?'

I blink. A bird zooms out of the chewing-gum world and begins circling my head. Clumsy, it lands on my shoulder, but when I go to pet it, it disappears. The sound of its beating wings lingers a moment, and then the void of its disappearance remains. I remember I have lungs. I take a long breath in. I also remember I have a name.

'Taking a long breath in doesn't mean you're concentrating,' the psychic says.

'Then how do I do it?'

'Concentrating!' she repeats. 'Fucking hell.'

I breathe in again, trying to think of nothing. Some minutes pass. I inhale. I exhale.

'Furrowing your brow won't do it, babe,' she says. 'You could just about try fooling someone in primary school in this shitty way.'

The Half-dead Plants

After the summer, I found a new flat, and during one of my first visits I asked the outgoing tenant if she'd been happy living there. She said she'd been very happy. They were the same rooms in which she had broken up with her husband, but there had certainly been much happiness there too. She was even happy about the end of her marriage. We laughed together. Her face looked sad from the forehead to the nose, but happy and relaxed from the mouth to the chin. Two different moods inhabited the same face and the same woman. The end of her marriage had been an ending, but one that made her happy. Her ending had also been a beginning in a maxillofacial sense.

'I can't take the plants from the terrace to my new place. Do you want to buy them from me?' she asked.

'Sure,' I said.

Later, as autumn unfolded, her half-dead plants would become my half-dead plants, and the flat in which her marriage had ended would be the flat I moved into, after my own marriage did. The former tenant was happier than me now, at least in the lower half of her face.

In the new flat, we knocked down a couple of walls, re-painted, fixed everything that needed fixing, and then my husband moved both his boxes and my boxes in. Clearly, we hadn't been very straightforward with one another. Above all, we didn't feel sure about a single thing, and this had meant leaving our previous home in a bad state and in a hurry. We, too, felt split in two: forehead-to-nose, nose-to-chin. We were saying goodbye to each other, while we assembled our new flatpack chairs. We were buying new plants that were already half dead.

'Why did you bring your things here?' I asked him on the evening we moved in.

It was winter. All our thoughts were ice-cold. There wasn't one single square centimetre of floor free for us to collapse on, and rest. It was clear he was moving into my flat, but I, too, had chosen to ignore it. It was easier to measure out together the new kitchen, the tables, our bed. It was difficult to let go of the dreams from before, the habits we had shaped together. Our books, our pillows, our baby. Carrying boxes was easier by joining our arms together. Our arms, together, were the place where Nico wanted to be. The circle of my own arms, alone, was much smaller.

'Let's take it easy,' he said. 'And anyway, I still haven't found a place for myself.'

'How do we deal with stuff, till that happens?'

We decided we'd spend a week each in the new flat, so Nico would have some degree of continuity: between us, we could deal with it – there were trips we needed to take, work and the welcoming houses of friends. The break-up would be our secret, and for the time being, we needn't tell Nico anything. We'd take turns to leave in the evening, while he was asleep, and come back the following morning, before breakfast. Other times, we could tell him we were off on a work trip for a few days. We'd always travelled a lot, since Nico was born, and so the plan could really work. We didn't know yet how to tell him that we were about to split up. We couldn't explain why. Often, we rehearsed the sentences we would say, but they always felt like lies, or too complicated for him to understand. Sometimes, the sentences we rehearsed made us laugh.

'Let's tell him that our home will be bigger, because it's made up of two flats.'

'And all the streets and the gardens in between are part of it.'

'Let's just tell him we don't love each other anymore.'

'That's not true, that we don't love each other anymore. It's a different kind of love.'

'So let's tell him we love each other with a different kind of love, but we are no longer a couple.'

'He's four.'

We said 'he's four' after nearly every sentence. Sometimes this meant Nico was old enough to understand, and sometimes it meant he was so young that he wouldn't.

My husband and I were going to therapy in order to split up without fighting and find the right sentence to say to Nico. We were going to a place called Gea – *Genitori Ancora* – 'Still

39

Parents'. This was true: we would be parents forever, and, more than therapy, going to Gea felt like one interminable dress rehearsal for a one-night-only, sad show, whose sole audience would be our son. Yet we kept going, because we also needed to find the right sentence for our own sake. We, too, were the audience, and our families, and our friends, and, if one wished to exaggerate, the whole world out there. Have you ever actually investigated truth? Is there even such a thing as truth? Are you good or bad? If we are mortal, why bother with such an immortal leap of faith? Will the half-dead plants survive in the end? We couldn't be shallow or too quick. We needed to understand things, and once we'd understood them, we needed to be able to clearly communicate our findings. It was like finding the right beginning for a new story, but both the writer and the editor – us – were uncertain which storyline would hold the reader in thrall, sell more copies, deliver a better ending, and anyway the publishing market was plummeting. In the beginning, and for a long time, the questions we kept asking were always the same. Where did we go wrong? Were we guilty? I could have been better. He could have been better. But we hadn't been – so how could we be better now? When we realised how many sentences would need to follow that initial one, it hit us hard. We hadn't thought about that yet. We hadn't considered that, even if we broke up, we could never break up for real, because of Nico, and so what hadn't worked out between us as lovers would continue not working, even after we broke up. We needed to break up without losing each other, and this two-way movement felt both contradictory and unnatural.

Go away forever! Stay forever! Look at me! Never look at me again! I began to understand the face of my flat's former tenant a little better: sad, all the way down to the nose; happy, nose to chin.

We carried on like this for a while, taking turns in the flat overnight, and trying out sentences in the day. The plan was working, one way or another, though our boxes remained stacked in some of the rooms, and neither of us was ever going grocery shopping. Our wash bags were filled and then emptied. I left the flat with a fresh pair of panties and my toothbrush in my purse. When it was my turn to stay at a hotel, I stole miniature jams and honey for Nico, who liked them. During those months, I also stole countless toothbrushes, shampoos and conditioners, and Nico thought I was buying them at the beauty counter and loved lining them up in the bathroom. I was tired; it was impossible to write in any structured way. It was painful having to leave the flat with the moped on a frosty evening, and painful to pick it up again when dawn came. Sometimes my husband and I cried, sometimes we fought; other times everything felt normal and just the same, and it seemed like it could last forever. We thought we had been a beautiful couple. Could we be a beautiful family now, even apart? Was our family, and having a baby, what killed us? And what role did this entail for Nico?

'You can hug me a little longer if you want?' we'd take turns in saying, because in turns we felt the need to hug the other a little longer, but in turns we were afraid we would kiss, which would have meant losing sight of the reality of their situation. When I got close to him, I didn't know if I hoped to feel something or nothing at all. Both options frightened me. Slowly, our hugs changed their shape, and his arms acquired a different kind of resistance. He could no longer save me, and I could no longer trust what I would find in him. Sometimes, instead of his arms, I met the void; sometimes he met my cheeks with his lips, in place of my mouth. Quickly, we became other from what we used to be. Hugs disappeared and I learnt to keep my distance. We had new names for our new roles, new words for our new fears.

'Why don't you look at me while I'm talking?' I'd ask.

Over the years, I had pronounced this same sentence many times. By then, though, I had at least an idea: he didn't know if, meeting my eyes, he would find his beloved, or a stranger.

'Have you watered the half-dead plants?' I insisted. And he never had.

We never slept next to each other again. Never again did we hug in bed. We never said I love you again. He never asked me to get back together, and I never asked him to come back to me. We'd been a couple for fifteen years and our bodies had fitted together for fifteen years. I had been sleeping with him since I was nineteen. He'd been my life and I'd been his. We'd changed a thousand homes together, and cities, habits, bars, restaurants, jobs, friends. Together, we'd travelled all over the world, followed our urges, learnt new songs and how to use each new computer. We'd watched films old and new, and talked about books, the times we lived in and what was happening in America, in Egypt, in Beirut. We had loved each other madly and nothing in particular had happened, if not for the fact that our love had ended. At the same time, everything had happened: his lies about cheating, and mine, freedom that had turned into the freedom of being away from each other, and not the freedom of coming together; our total collapse in the face of a mutual project: a son and a new idea of us that had more to do with dedication and care. The rest of our lives. Life. Death. Summer and winter. Everything and nothing.

'Perhaps this could be a way to fall in love with each other again, at some point in the future,' we'd said in the beginning.

Meanwhile, I was looking for suitable homes for him, and kept finding our photobooth pictures with 'I'll love you forever' scrawled on the back in my wallet. Sometimes, I looked through our eyes from before: mine, through which I had watched him and loved him; his, through which he'd loved me.

'Here, it's your love you are looking at!' I would tell him then.

If I went through our emails on the wrong night, I cried. Some of them were so full of love. Some of them thick with attempts to understand each other and make up. Making up. Making up had used to work, but now it wasn't about that. When I searched for a home for him, sometimes he'd get angry and say, 'I don't like how proactive you are in kicking me out of the flat.' Other times he would thank me.

'You haven't been taking good care of me,' I often told him.

'You haven't been taking good care of me,' he often told me.

From the terrace, the half-dead plants stared, as if to say: and now nobody's taking care of us, OK?

In those days, Maria had finally left hospital and was beginning her rehabilitation programme. It was more than rehabilitation for her: she needed to learn how to come back to life. She didn't have any particular task or daily routine to follow. She had to get up in the morning. Breathe. Try not to think that her next breath could be her last. Get used to being very tired. Have patience. Inhabit the void of her days with no work and no strength. Make her bed. Get back into it.

Alessandro had also just left hospital. One of his hands hadn't recovered well, and many other parts of his body didn't work as they'd used to before the accident. His sight was gone in one eye and his hips were still held in place by various screws. His vision would permanently remain out of focus: he had to make peace with loving a stain. There was a little balloon inside his aorta and less hair on his head. After all those months in the hospital, he and Diana had broken up once and for all in September and she'd moved her clothes out of their flat.

Months later, when Alessandro told me about the accident – which I'd only known about from the bar onwards, and then that fateful bend... – he began with the day before the one I thought of as 'day zero'. Or what the psychic and everyone else knew as the Day of the Disaster. Alessandro is a good storyteller. Sometimes, his voice is a little unsteady, sometimes he words things strongly, and he can really make you laugh.

That day, the minus-one day, or day one, or twenty three thousand two hundred and one, in the year two thousand and something, or year zero of the Palaeocene, he was working as set director for a TV ad in Rome. They'd been shooting in a mega villa on the Appia Antica and after they had wrapped things up, he had slept in the bed that had hosted a famous film star just a few hours earlier.

In those days, he and my sister had broken up, so he had taken a girl back to the villa. In the morning he woke up next to the pool and bumped into Woody Allen.

'The villa, Woody Allen, summer. I was definitely on a fake high, but it was also a high from the pain of the end of our love. Anyway, I felt really great that day.'

That afternoon, Alessandro had travelled back to Milan. In the evening, he'd attended a concert and drank two beers. He'd gone to meet his old-time friend Tommaso in a different bar, taking the ring road to get there. He'd got drunk at Tommaso's bar, vodka on top of beer, and from then on, he couldn't really remember.

'I remember the route because I figured it out later, in my imagination. I've done that trip thousands of times. Tommaso was riding his motorbike next to me. We might have even been racing each other like two idiots. The most amazing thing isn't that I didn't get the bend right, but that I cut straight through it at a speed of a hundred and twenty. It makes me wonder whether I'd meant to kill myself, and if I'm honest, I'm still not sure I hadn't.'

What's for sure is that it was Diana he was thinking about when he found himself on the ground, and still her whom he'd wanted by the side of his hospital bed. Tommaso assisted him. Alessandro was bleeding from the mouth and the nose. The ambulance came and, in his mind, the memory is associated with panic.

'I felt no pain. My hips were split open, but I couldn't feel anything,' he said.

While Alessandro was being checked into hospital – still on an orange alert code as they hadn't yet spotted his torn vein – Tommaso got back on his bike and went straight to Alessandro's parents' house and rang the bell.

'That's the best thing he ever did for me in his life,' Alessandro told me. 'He didn't call. He went to see them.'

Living in the Desert

After Alessandro's accident, Maria's brain aneurysm and the end of my love, my brother Teo got married in a ceremony held at my mother's art gallery. We all dressed up for it. We ate Puglian food, danced and drank. My sister Allegra flew in from New Zealand. Our uncles and aunties said that the chicory with fava beans had been perfectly cooked; my son Nico was wearing a little tie and danced with my mother. My grandmother was thrilled with the wedding and the fact that they had chosen to celebrate it there. As usual, she was elegantly dressed, standing out in her bedecked factory, a ring on each finger and lipstick on her lips. We all said, 'Grandad would've been thrilled,' and I was very sad that day that my grandfather hadn't had a chance to meet our kids and had never read any of my books. We could have printed one on his Roland Ultra, even. Why had I chosen to use my father's surname, instead of his and my mother's, on the cover of my novels? Now, once my mother died, her surname would be lost forever. She was the last of the line: my grandfather had been the son of orphaned provincial railroad workers and his surname had been made up in the registrar's office. He was born very poor and became very rich. He'd been a partisan during World War II, then married my grandmother – the beautiful, blonde daughter of a local seamstress – and loved her deeply for the rest of his life. His love letters to her are romantic and well written. My grandad had collected contemporary art, crossed the Atlantic Ocean in his boat, bought land in Brazil and the Antilles. He'd visited the world's best museums, eaten in all the best restaurants in Paris, Capri and New York, owned fast cars, slept in luxury hotels and spent his evenings playing cards and drinking fine bottles of wine with his friends. He'd been a good grandad and a good father. And then he'd died at seventy-two, in my grandmother's and my sister Allegra's arms.

'She's an artist,' my grandad used to say about me to my mother, because I'd given him a gouache painting when I was in primary school, which he'd thought was very well balanced in colour and space. He'd hung it in his bedroom, next to a real Dalí.

'Our love was a rollercoaster,' my grandmother told me at the wedding. 'But your grandad never cheated on me: I was the only person he told everything. He couldn't keep a secret from me if he'd wanted to.' I remembered it differently: that my grandmother had known about some of the cheating and had been very angry about it. Maybe she'd forgotten it all, or maybe she'd decided it was fine in the end: memory isn't much use in some situations, especially when it forces you to remain angry. A part of me wished I was more like her. What's anger got to do with life and death anyway?

'Your father wasn't there for you,' Grandma added. I was about to defend him, but I took another sip of wine instead. 'Not in the same way as your grandfather was there.'

'So? Where's your father?' the psychic whispers in London. 'You're tired of this absence!' she adds. Is she impersonating my grandmother?

'OK, OK,' I say. I want to ask her when she found out she was a psychic, and whether it was similar to discovering any other vocation, like being a dancer, a writer or a doctor. Her eyes are sparkling, her teeth perfect, her nail polish pink.

'What do you want to ask me?' she says again. 'I can tell you now you'll have trouble with your knees, and a daughter. Rain will return and everything will sprout new leaves. Now concentrate, shut up and go back to where you were.'

So I have to go back to the heat and the half-dead plants, while in my head I resolve to take better care of my knees. I run a finger over one of my knees, then the other, and cross my fingers.

'Uncross your fingers! What do you think you're doing?' the psychic says, and I do as she says. What do I think I'm doing?

Maria was also among the wedding guests. It was her first public outing since the aneurysm. Her hair was shaved, her gaze both lost and new at the same time. She, too, had new eyes and a new body with which to inhabit the Earth. Her birthday fell on the same day as the wedding, so around 11 p.m. a large jam tart with cream had arrived for her. I took it, or somebody put it in my hands. Anyway, in my memory, I am going towards her with the lit candles, while over a hundred people sing Happy Birthday. Maria blew out the candles, and when I hugged her, my heart began to beat faster. I couldn't let go of her, but I couldn't say anything. We hadn't spoken since the day of the aneurysm. Was she angry with me because I had never called her? Was she having a bad time this evening? I was angry with myself for not calling, and not visiting her in hospital while she was a patient.

I stayed there, clinging onto Maria's neck, in the same courtyard in which her vein had exploded. Perhaps we were even standing in the very same square centimetre. We were standing in the same place where my grandfather had given me books as a gift. Where I'd told my mother about the end of my love. Where my mother wanted to open Pong, the ping-pong venue. We were standing at the beginning of something new, next to something that had ended forever. Maria was turning thirty today, and she was alive. My brother was getting married. Nico was laughing. My grandmother was happy. Over those past few months I had been taking care uniquely of my own self. I hadn't had to worry about learning to walk again, plus everything else, putting one foot in front of the other. Maria had had to. And so had Alessandro.

'Thank you for calling the ambulance,' she said.

She'd told my mother I had saved her. I didn't feel like I'd saved her at all, so it was a strange kind of gratitude to receive.

'How are you?' I asked.

'Anyone else wouldn't have believed me, but you did, and that made them come quicker.'

Maria was more fragile, and simultaneously harder, than she had been before the aneurysm. She smiled, ate the cake and kissed her boyfriend. I knew him, because he was a gardener and had helped me transfer my grandmother's plants onto my new terrace. My grandmother had just moved too, and she no longer needed the leaves and the branches that had sheltered her and my grandfather. She no longer needed my grandad's bed, and she didn't need my grandad's clothes, or the space necessary to house two grandparents. She needed space for herself, to begin to weigh less, own less, see less. As I held Maria, I wondered how often she thought about death. Whether she was thinking about it as she took this very breath. And then this next breath, and the one after that. It was a quick, precise thought. Then I rephrased it: how often could she go *without* thinking of death? I rephrased it again: how long could I? And my grandmother? My mother? What about all of the people at this party and on Earth?

'Can I have Grandad's bed?' I'd asked my grandmother.

'Of course,' she'd said. 'Take anything you like.'

'I'm taking Grandad's bed off Grandma's hands,' I said to my mother at the wedding.

'You always want everything,' she commented.

'Do you never want anything?'

Alessandro also came to the wedding; it was his first outing
since hospital too. His hair had thinned at the nape of his
neck, because of the many months he'd spent lying down,
and one of his arms had become very thin and had lost
some mobility. He was still himself, but it felt as if he were
speaking to us from a faraway place. There were at least
ten glass panes between his face, his body and the rest of
the world. His smiles were tight. He was tired. Months
later I read what Alessandro had been carrying around
that evening, written all over his hospital discharge papers:

*Craniofacial trauma, with contusive-haemorrhagic frontopolar right
lesion. Frontal hemosinus. Facial trauma. Malar bone fracture, right.
Fracture of the zygomatic arch, right, not gull-winged. Maxillary
sinus fracture, right, anterior and lateralposterior wall, displaced and
pluri-fragmented. Maxillary sinus fracture, left, lateralposterior wall,
compound. Fracture of the pterygoid processes. Orbital fracture, right,
lateral wall, left, in correspondence of the frontal-zygomatic suture,
moderately displaced. Orbital fracture, left, medial wall, compound,
with presence of small air bubbles. Fractured nose, septum, multi-
fragmented, proper bones, with extension to the pyramid and left
root, jaw fracture, right, branch, involving the coranoid. Cervical
trauma. Thoracic trauma, with atelectasis and pleural effusion, both
right and left, and in the apical pneumothorax flap, right. Periaortic
hematoma. Acute aortic syndrome. Intimal flap in descending aorta
via metatraumatic dissection. Aortic endoprosthesis. Fracture of the
ilio-pubic bone, left. Inguinal hematoma, left. Radius fracture, left,
metaepiphyseal, multi-fragmented, and of the ulna, left and the*

styloid (Smith-Goyrand fracture). Brachial plexus suffering, left.

Lots of stuff, is what I mean. And it was all uniquely his, for him alone to carry.

'How are you doing?' I asked him too.

'Really well,' he said. He could have gone through the whole above-mentioned list and so he was probably being sarcastic, but at the same time he wasn't. He was really well, he was alive. He wasn't so well, he'd nearly died. There was modesty in highlighting his own transformation, which I perceived. Just as I understood his attempt to act as if nothing had ever happened, as if he were exactly the same as before, and on the other hand his urge for a constant reminder of everything he had gone through, and which shouldn't be blocked out by us, nor him. He was on a different level of awareness, of fear, of sense. That level was denied to us, and it must have felt lonely for him to know that he existed on the other side of a wall. How does one reach out to people? I thought. How would my neighbour's and my grandmother's plants get on, on the terrace? And me, alone, in grandfather's bed? I did my best to be warm to everybody. A little while later, I went back to dancing and took a picture with my sisters and my brother. In the photograph we're all holding a drink and pulling silly faces. My tongue's sticking out as if I'm saying *aah*. Behind us, you can see the Roland Ultra, the largest printing machine in my grandfather's factory, in my mother's gallery, and the largest one in the world, at least in my heart.

Cleaning Out the Dead Leaves

That night, and the ones that followed, I slept little. I handed in the first draft of a novel I'd finished some time back. I was working for TV and magazines, filling my days to the point I had to write lists of what I needed to do all over my hands. Sometimes I filled them up to the wrists. I was writing about a couple's break-up for a TV series, and in a virtuous and vicious cycle many of our words – the conversations between my husband and I – kept ending up in the mouths of the actors. I made those actors break up and argue like us. I gave him my husband's tics, and her, mine. So one evening I saw an actress on the telly say the same words I had said to my husband. She was looking at the actor who played her husband, asking: 'Have you run out of care for me? Why don't you ever look in my eyes?' For ten whole minutes I watched us play out on the screen. My hair was curly, and I had blue eyes. The actress was crying and so was I. Nico was sleeping in a flat where my husband no longer lived. I already knew how it was going to end up in real life, and I knew how it was going to end up on the telly. In the middle of the night, I sent a text message to the actress, thanking her – she'd been so great. I sent another text to my husband, but he didn't reply.

'Are you writing?' my mother asks all the time, as she's been asking forever.

'I'm writing,' I say.

Though in those months I wasn't writing in the way she meant. I was editing the novel that was about to come out, and I was writing on commission, for others. But I wasn't writing how I was supposed to write, no. I wasn't doing that. I was taking care of practical things, work, distractions. At home, for instance, I'd been hanging up old pictures on new walls, and, out of the house, I had taken to exploring our new neighbourhood. On the terrace, I had checked the old irrigation system and put my grandmother's plants next to previous tenant's. They were all mine now, and they were all connected.

'How are my plants doing?' my grandmother would ask on the phone.

'Really well,' I lied.

How are my plants doing? my flat's former tenant texted.

They're looking happy, I exaggerated.

Before the real cold arrived, I tried to do to the plants the little I knew I should do to them. I cleaned out the dead leaves, I watered them. Then we all left together – my sisters, my brother and his wife, Nico, my mother and my grandmother – to a place in the countryside that my mother had rented for the weekend. On Sunday morning, my brother announced that he and his wife were expecting a baby. It was sunny, we hugged. The first thing I thought was that they might break up because of this baby. I corrected myself, thinking of all the couples that were still able to love each other, even after they had children. Could my husband and I love one another again, in a thousand days, a thousand months, a thousand years? Was this simply winter?

Nico and I were sleeping on a tatami in front of a window that gave onto the woods. In the evenings, I held him and synchronised my breathing to his. My mother had told me that whenever you have trouble falling asleep, you should put your hand on the arm of someone who's sleeping, and they'll transfer the sleep onto you. She used to do it with us as children, and I do it with Nico. On the second evening, while I was trying this technique out, holding onto him to fall asleep, he wet the bed. A little pee went on me, and the rest on the tatami.

When she found out, the owner was deeply offended.

'I'm so sorry,' I said.

'It will rot,' she said. And I took even this sentence as a condemnation of me.

Over those months, my mother had been drifting away from me, because of my decision to pursue a divorce. Whenever we argued, the grave expression on her face as she asked me if I was sure of my choice irritated me. I hated that she wouldn't ask if I had been unhappy in my marriage, and whether I was feeling happier these days. I hated that she assumed it was all my fault. How could she know that, if I didn't? Her manner of imagining our future and recalling our past felt like a threat to me.

'He gave Nico his bottle when he was a baby,' she said.

'I breastfed him for ten months,' I retaliated.

'What's that got to do with it?'

'What's with the feeding Nico with bottles, then?'

Over the same months my mother had finalised her divorce from my father, after a long separation lasting seventeen years, and the coincidence of all this breaking up and losing people had left her somewhat bereft. When they'd first broken up for real, I'd been the only one to know. It was summer, my seventeenth, and I'd found out while I was away on a theatre retreat. I'd called my mother, and she'd been in tears. She'd told me: 'We've broken up, but don't tell anyone. Not even your brother and sisters.' Partly owing to the theatre retreat, partly to what she'd told me, that evening I shaved off all my hair. I looked very ugly.

Now we could finally talk about the end of her love again, and mine, and Diana's. We could talk about jellyfish and the end of the world. It was a mutual grievance: mine, hers and the planet's. We could have stuck our complaints into the mouth of any person in the universe, and it would have more or less worked, would have sounded more or less honest. It was all the same to me, then. Life; death. Look at me. Never look at me again. Leave me alone, never leave me. The desert. The forest.

'Your father never changed a single nappy, and there were four of you to care for,' my mother insisted.

'So what?' I asked.

'Talking to you is impossible.'

'I think it's impossible to talk in the way you mean talking,' I said.

'So, write.'

'Do you think you won't be loved if you don't write?' the psychic asks me in London.

'If I don't write, I'll be punished,' I say. I smile. I'm still holding the pink quartz. Her mouth is a centimetre away from my face and my ear.

'It's not like I buy that you're actually happy just because you're smiling,' she says. To demonstrate, she repeats the same sentence while laughing. Then pretending to cry. Acting as if she were about to die. Having an orgasm.

'OK! OK!' I say to make her stop. 'I get it!'

'You get me or you?' she asks. She's starting to piss me off.

'I will survive,' she goes on. 'Even if I piss you off. I won't die from it. Quite the opposite. I'll carry on being very hungry, for anything, all the time. Even fried tripe or steamed tongue. So, chill.'

'I'm chill,' I say.

'Then why are you shaking?'

My mother maintained she'd never go back. She also maintained she could have been better and then maybe her marriage would have worked out. She was both nostalgic and resentful. There was still a lot of love between them too. They'd gone back to each other so many times over their long separation; their faces had laughed and cried at the same time, while their bodies and their minds had wished for opposite things. My father had told me: your mother didn't want to get back together with me. My mother had told me: your father didn't want to be somebody's lover.

'Are you sad?' I asked my mother.

'I'm alone,' my mother said.

I hadn't accounted for the fact that, in saying goodbye to my husband, my mother would also have to say goodbye to him, to some extent. She'd seen him grow up. If I left him, my brother also had to leave him, and my sisters, and my mother and everyone else in my life. In a way, it was as if he had to die. Even my father had kind of died when he had separated from my mother. Who'd seen him since? Who'd ever received a cuddle from him since? He never called me; I never saw him.

My sister Diana, my mother and I, like most people on Earth, carried on like that for a while, backwards and forwards, in the middle of all these endings. All phone conversations among the women of the family revolved around the same subject at the time, and they were getting repetitive. My brother, who on the other hand had just got married and was expecting a daughter, was happy. And anyway, he was a man, so we involved him less in our business.

'She'll get tired, make sure to help her out,' I told him.

He said of course he would do that, that he just couldn't wait. As kids, us sisters had convinced him that his willy would fall off when he grew up, as had happened to all three of us, so of course we could teach him how to help out his wife. He did help her, thankfully. Which is another reason why us sisters haven't made his willy fall off, yet.

The First Tiny Seed

On one of those days of half-dead plants, I ran into Maria. She was getting better, but she was still feeling scared. She told me about the psychotherapy sessions she was undergoing.

'You don't come out the same when you've looked death right in the face like I have,' she told me.

Her therapy was similar to that administered to sufferers of PTSD, and in fact her psychologist also treated soldiers who had fought in Afghanistan and Iraq. His studio was a few paces away from my new flat.

'Sometimes I feel bad,' Maria said. 'If I think about it, that day, and the sickness… it's like a liquid substance rising up and enveloping me completely.'

My tears ran into the pouches under my eyes and stopped there.

'I just don't feel safe anymore,' she added.

Around us, many things in the world looked ugly. The graffiti on the walls. The supermarket, its signs stomped out by vandals. The access route to the dingy underground parking lot. The rubbish that people had ditched on the ground: dirty plastics and soiled napkins. And we didn't look that good ourselves. We talked about that and felt sad that so many people didn't try to live a better life and be kind to others.

Maria and her boyfriend ran a sort of plant nursery. Together, they organised guerrilla gardening operations, planting flowers without permission to brighten up the city.

'I don't like it when people do it at night – as if there's anything to hide. But anyway, people always steal the flowers.'

'Really?' I said. 'Do they always do that?'

'If you use lesser-known flowers, they don't steal them. If you plant cyclamens, they steal them straightaway. Peonies are quite well known, but not enough. So they don't steal them.'

My first, tiny illumination came in that moment, and in that moment, Maria gave me the first tiny seed. I didn't even know it was a seed, then.

'Are you going back to work?' I asked.

'No,' she said. Our two solitudes saw one another and patted each other on the back.

That evening, I dined with Diana. We sat on the terrace, drinking a beer. She was still in love with Alessandro, and yet she wasn't. Alessandro was still in love with her, and yet he wasn't. They were the same as before. They were different from before. We all had a 'before' to refer back to now. The fact that they'd never gone to the Philippines really bothered both of them. I had the same problem with Japan.

'You should ask Maria to help you with your plants,' she said. 'They look really ill.'

'They're not adjusting well,' I mumbled.

'You don't give them enough water. They have too little soil. Their leaves are yellow. They need feeding.'

'Isn't that right for them to have yellow leaves?'

She smiled as if I'd made a joke. The plants didn't look well, indeed. Like most people, I wanted the plants all around me, but I wasn't capable of making them spread. I only desired the plants superficially. I watered them, but not enough. I watered them in the way I was taught at three years of age: a little in the morning, a little in the evening, for a little bit.

'Ask Maria to help you,' my sister repeated.

I nodded, but for several weeks afterwards I forgot that I'd nodded. I watched the plants die and it didn't affect me. Forgetting about things, or people, didn't affect me.

Around that time, I found a place for my husband near mine, on the other side of the small park. After some renovation to the property, he moved in. That night I ended up in hospital, the same one they had taken Alessandro to, months earlier. My stomach had shrunk so much that I wasn't able to breathe, and in the morning I came back home full of love for hospitals and painkillers. On the discharge papers, the doctor had written, the patient shows 'emotional lability'. When I got home, I struck through the 'L' with a pen: the patient shows 'emotional ability'.

As well as a flat for my husband, we'd also finally found the right sentence to say to our son, and it was one that could work even when followed by all the other sentences. Therapy hadn't lasted for very long, and anyway the whole time we'd been at pains to explain to the therapist that we weren't angry. It was a kind of boasting.

'You shouldn't spend a lot of time together,' the therapist would say.

'What if it comes naturally to us?' my husband asked.

'It won't come naturally to you. Otherwise, why are you breaking up?'

'We're not like the others,' my husband insisted. 'You can't know that, but it's true.'

That man must have heard the same sentence so many times. If I had been in the mood, I could have come up with a long, precise list in answer to his question. I had a million tiring replies ready in order to come across as a better person than I actually was. Instead, all I was doing was swallowing sand. Cleaning my glasses. Drying my tears. Living in the desert.

We were in the middle of moving the last few boxes from my flat to my husband's new place when I first saw my future new boyfriend. We were in a restaurant. I was sitting with a friend when he walked past us. He and I exchanged a few words. He was tall, wide-shouldered, smiling. My heart started beating faster. I kept smiling, and I know that I also thought, immediately, 'I love you,' and as soon as I did, I hurled that thought and that sentence a thousand miles away from myself. When he turned around, and continued walking, I made a hex that I would never see him again. I tried to think 'farewell', instead of what I'd thought earlier.

'What just happened?' I said to my friend.

Later on, in the afternoon, my legs were still shaking, and I felt restless. I was convinced that anything happening between me and another man could only ever be an imaginary oasis in the middle of the desert. I worried I'd be eating more sand, instead of drinking water, and that I wouldn't be capable of walking across the dunes to check if it was all a mirage. The hallucinations I was experiencing, anyway, were probably a consequence of my emotional lability, which must have also prompted my thinking 'I love you' within seven seconds of meeting somebody.

I made a resolution and spoke it out loud: 'If I never see him again, we'll all be safe.'

As soon as I had made this resolution, my heartbeat finally calmed down.

When I received his first message, I didn't reply.

To the second, I answered: 'Not now, but it is evident we'll have to deal with this at some point.' My heart was rushing again. I remembered how terrible I was at sticking to the resolutions I made, and thought about my poor heart, which hadn't been so healthy lately.

'Did you ever hear from him again?' my friend asked me, now and then.

'Never again,' I said, as if it were a sign of strength.

But I kept seeing his smiling mouth in my mind; I wrote his name down on paper and imagined him writing mine. In my imagination, he wrote my name in even bigger letters, even more times. Sometimes, he doodled flowers next to it.

For Nico's day of truth, my husband and I planned everything in detail. We would tell him at my place. We'd eat together out on the terrace, good food that he liked, and that we wouldn't need to force him to eat. So, no fish or green vegetables. Then we'd go over to my husband's flat to see his new bedroom, and together we would make our son's new bed. Nico wouldn't stay there for another few weeks, but he would learn, for now, that the other bed existed, and that his father's flat was another place he could call his and sleep in. We'd call the flats by the name of the street, rather than Mum's flat and Dad's flat. We tried to imagine a huge house that comprised both sets of rooms and even the trees and the cafe in between, the one we liked to stop at for coffee in the morning.

'We are only an open-air corridor away from each other,' we concluded.

Our son looked at us and said he was hungry. We repeated to him that we were no longer married, no longer husband and wife, but that we would all love each other forever, nonetheless.

'Can we eat?' he repeated.

We were hungry too. Thank God there was no fish or green veg. We went out to the terrace and had lunch there. It was sunny and the plants barely shaded us because they were half dead. As we walked from one flat to the other, Nico held a toy guitar in his hands and we were certainly still a family, walking together towards the same place. My husband and I were crying under our sunglasses, but in the middle of all that sadness we were also happy, because we were doing things properly and we were certain that Nico would be forever and equally looked after, despite the fact of this open-air corridor, right in the middle of our living space.

We held each other's hands; we smiled.

The following week, Nico's nursery teachers told me that he'd been a little restless lately, but that over the past week he seemed to have finally found his place.

'What do you mean, his place?' I asked.

'Physically, he's able to sit still in the same place. Mentally, he seems in a good place. He's fine.'

'A week ago, his father and I told him we are splitting up,' I said.

'A week ago, exactly?' the older teacher asked.

'Exactly,' I said.

The two teachers looked at each other and nodded. Bingo, their eyes said. They were nodding as if to say, see what children are like, and smiling because, once again in their long career, they'd been right. They looked as if they were about to high five. I felt guilty for the time we'd kept Nico in the dark. We'd thought we were being good, but had we been bad? I felt ashamed, even in front of the teachers. It was the first bad thing Nico had discovered about life, and we had imparted it to him. His first bout of pain came from us. But did this at least mean that pain, like fear, like love and death, was another thing we got to teach him, and so the fact that it came from us made it ultimately better?

'Until a week ago, he was jumping from one game to the next, he just couldn't settle. He was restless. Nervy. Now he's better.'

How afraid had Nico been at night? And in the day at school, when he couldn't settle? What was troubling him? Thinking about it, was it strictly necessary that he went to school at all? Why didn't I simply hold him in my arms all the time? I was overcome by the need to wrap him around my body and travel the world with him. I wanted to go to Japan!

'Sorry,' I said.

My diaphragm had closed up; I swallowed more saliva, breathed deeper.

'Children are incredible,' the younger teacher repeated.

'We're not angry – I mean, with each other. We wanted you to know that,' I added.

'Well, that's good,' the teachers said, awkwardly.

'Do you have any advice?' I asked.

I was ready to accept advice from anyone, on anything: on sleeping better at night, on how to cook pasta, on how to be a better mother and writer. Could anyone help me save my plants from dying? To be more present with my grandmother and everyone else?

'There are parents here who drop off their children at school like parcels. They don't talk to each other for months, and we are like a parking lot to them, so they can drop their kids off before they run away. You two don't seem to have that problem.'

'We're getting on, yeah,' I said. 'We're not like the others.'

In that moment, I was four years old, just like Nico. We all smiled. I loved everyone in that room, and I was suddenly grateful for my country, state schools, teachers, broken chairs that had been mended, all human beings and us three, together still, at that time, trying to make sad things work out in the best possible way. Looking after our children, and their education, and a future that would hopefully be fairer on them.

When I told my mother about all the things we were trying to be – separate, but close by, apart, but on each other's side – she said the same thing the therapist had said: 'I hope so, but I'm not sure that could ever happen.'

'What are we meant to do, then?' I asked.

'In this situation, one of you two will inevitably end up suffering more.'

'But we're not angry,' I told her too. 'We're not like the others.'

Water Came Back from the Sky

'I can hear the sound of pages being turned,' I say.

'Are you hypnotised yet?' the psychic asks.

'I don't know. Am I?'

'Are the pages in the present or in the past?'

I remain silent. How does one tell if they're in the present or in the past?

'I was drawing your tarot. You're in love.'

I see that the psychic is looking at my cards, but also simultaneously at a large cookery book. The book is open at the curry section. I shut my eyes again.

'This new love could be so beautiful, but the thing is, you don't trust anyone and you're always thinking about something else,' she says. 'I see an airship.'

'In the cards?'

'I keep seeing this airship, and you, struggling to find a parking space for it.'

The image is so funny I laugh.

'You're laughing now, but it'll take a lot of focus to find

a parking space for an airship, way more space than you've got now.' The airship appears in my mind too. It's silver and I'm holding onto it with a kite string. Wow!

'Why are you reading recipes?' I ask the psychic.

'I'm not reading recipes,' she answers, with surprise. 'Maybe you should figure out why you'd rather chat about recipes when you've got such a massive airship to park.'

I open my eyes and the recipe book has disappeared.

'See? You don't trust me,' the psychic concludes. As I'm about to close my eyes, I see the cookbook has appeared again.

A little while later, I bumped into my future boyfriend again in a shop. I was trying on dresses, and he sat down to watch me. His gaze was familiar, and at the same time completely new. When we said goodbye an hour later, I missed him immediately. I wrote to him. He left for London, where he lived. He left for several other places, where his work took him. Whenever we were apart, we wrote to each other. Then he came back, we got closer, we kissed. We wrote to each other thousands of times, until we left together, in secret – a secret we were keeping, above all, from ourselves. After we'd said goodbye, we kept writing to each other. I made a resolution to cancel the previous resolution I had made. Another resolution to stop making resolutions altogether.

'Come to me?' he'd say.

And I'd say yes. I told him what time I'd arrive, how long I would stay. Where we'd eat, where we'd go out walking. But I only booked flights you could cancel without paying a penalty fee. And I almost always cancelled them.

'You do realise that as soon as you mention your boy-friend you start running away?' the psychic says.

'What do you mean?'

'You don't go into much detail. You're just listing facts, moving on quickly. Basically, you can't write well about him.'

'Oh, right. Thanks a lot for that.'

'There's no point in getting offended. Write better. Don't run. Stay,' she says.

I close my eyes and the airship yanks at me. Ouch! I try to stabilise it, but it's much bigger and stronger than me, and made of better silver.

'Don't run!' the psychic shouts again.

I plant my feet, tense my abs, try to organise myself in my body and mind.

Meanwhile, the plants kept getting worse and Diana insisted I wrote to Maria. So I did.

'Hi Maria, how you doing? Are you able to care for the plants on my terrace? They need help.'

'Of course,' she replied. She added: 'I'll come when the rain stops.' I thought, what a good way to plan. And it meant that the water had come back from the sky – had I even noticed that? Maybe I could use that same sentence for anything in life. It had been raining, in fact, for weeks. The plants could drink to their hearts' content, and they were certainly doing better than they had under my own care. As for myself, there was no expectation for me to be happy while the rain continued to pour, as I may have been expected to be on a sunny day.

When Maria finally came, she was sad.

'I'll take a look around today, so we can decide what needs doing,' she said. I hugged her and shut the door behind us.

'What's up?' I asked.

'I broke up with my boyfriend.'

'Why?' Another ending. Here it was.

'He replaced me.'

There were several of us now who'd just broken up with someone. My sister Diana, my mother and her divorce, my flat's previous tenant, me, and now Maria. Possibly millions of people just over the past week.

'How are you?'

'I'm sad,' she said. 'And real fucking angry.'

We roamed from pot to pot, checking the plants on the lower balcony and on the terrace. I didn't want to intrude on her life, and so I didn't ask her any more questions.

'That's a photinia. And a cherry laurel. And that's a mulberry tree – a parasite, I'm afraid; it's invited itself to the party.'

I listened to Maria talk, but I couldn't memorise a single thing. I didn't even fully understand what she was pointing at with her finger. Photinia? And yet, each time she pointed at one of the plants, I felt it somewhat came alive, as if Maria had brought it into being by giving it a name. Hello, mulberry? Good morning, Anna here. She was introducing them to me: look, it's alive! It lives here with you. Does knowing this plant is an uninvited guest to your party make you look at them with new eyes? Do you like that, having an additional plant, or does it bother you that you didn't invite it or pick it yourself? If you look at it a little closer, you'll remember it. Don't walk past it without knowing its name. Isn't that what you'd do with a person?

'You don't have any flowers,' she noted.

I discovered this in the moment she said it. I had no flowers. Not even one.

'It's all green. There's no colour. Is that how you like it?' she asked.

It was all green, without colour. I didn't know if that was how I liked it. The plants had belonged to my former tenant, and my grandma before she traded them down to me. Now they were my plants. But I hadn't chosen anything and the few things I had done up to this point had been the wrong things.

'I think I'd like flowers,' I concluded, after I'd taken another look around me, and, vaguely, inside me.

'There are several corpses,' Maria added. 'The feijoa. The strawberry tree and the osmanthus have died, unfortunately. And the laurel isn't doing too well.'

Was it my fault? 'Corpses' was a word that dredged up guilt. This time, I was sure I'd been bad.

'I'm not great with plants,' I explained. I wanted to add I'd not been good with her, either, while she'd been in hospital. But I remained silent, going through words in my head: feijoa. Osmanthus.

'I'll come round once to begin with, to do a big clear-out. Move some of these plants out of the way. Uproot the corpses.'

'I'm worried that Nico will fall through the gaps.'

'Yeah. There are lots of holes.'

As we said that, standing by the holes, the terrace looked emptier than I'd ever seen it. I had emptied the terrace by saying out loud that it was empty, as if I'd pronounced a magic spell. Each of the holes and the gaps, like the plants themselves, now had a name and a story. Each hole could turn into an abyss.

'How are you?' Maria asked me.

'Better. But it's complicated,' I said.

'Nico?'

'His teachers say he has found his place. But I haven't found my own place yet. Would you like a coffee?'

We had a coffee and a glass of water. The flat wasn't finished yet, and bare electrical wires hung from the walls, where the light fixtures would be attached. We ate bitter chocolate.

'Your terrace gets the kind of sunlight that somebody should come up with, if it didn't already exist,' Maria said.

Her hair had grown out again. She still had a boy's haircut, but a boy with long hair. She'd lost weight. She'd make the plants grow again, she would grow her own hair long again.

'Is this your job now, then?' I asked.

'No. I'm just doing it for you.'

I smiled and I saw her mouth again, telling me: my head is exploding. Please, help.

A little while later, my husband also started seeing somebody. He said he was sorry. I accepted his apology, even though I wasn't sure what I was forgiving him for. We immediately started rehearsing how we would tell our son. This time, too, the key concept should be: we love each other, but we also love somebody else, and anyway, everyone loves *you*. So much. You're the most loved boy in the world and we will always be here for you. This is a family, too, and it is a big one. Look how many open-air corridors connect the rooms that we live in, and we own all of them! Look how many different, half-dead plants can fit on a single terrace! The map of the house we'd describe was getting funnier and funnier. My end, for instance, now included the city of London, where my new boyfriend lived, with his two children, as well as several airports, and Boeing 737s.

'He's four years old,' my husband and I kept saying, and again, we sometimes meant he's not old enough for this, and other times he's too old for this.

And anyway, he was about to turn five now, so we couldn't use that sentence forever.

'Don't you want to scream it now, how angry you were?' the psychic says. 'If you do go for it, I recommend you shout it like a marine.' I want to make her happy, so I shout: we were angry.

'Louder! You have no voice!' she says. And, to make her happy, I shout that I have no voice, in the voice of a marine.

That year, we'd all become a little poorer. No one survived the financial crash unscathed, even those of us who kept our jobs were working less and for less money. The city and the country seemed enveloped in a thick fog. Jobs were worse than they used to be, and so were the papers and the TV.

Fewer movies were being made. Friends who worked with local manufacturers told us that more and more workplaces were closing every day. Seven people redundant. Then seventeen. A whole family. Factories shut down. Houses stood empty. Crisis, crisis, crisis. There was nothing in the short and medium term that didn't point towards crisis. Resilience, penitence and crisis. Often our fathers went bankrupt, and it was somewhat harder to see our fathers get poorer than being poorer ourselves. While at the same time our fathers were probably thinking the opposite: it's one thing becoming poor, another withstanding the idea that our children have become even poorer! Our children, the children born poor to the poor children of the fathers who'd got poor, were going to worse schools, with good teachers often, but with no paper, pens or soap. Our friends were leaving their homes for smaller flats, in neighbourhoods further away from the city. Everything we'd invested in and everything that our parents had invested in – hours and years of study, dreams, languages, books and travels, working since the age of eighteen or nineteen, our excellent academic degrees – none of that was paying back. All those dreams and that money and that energy had gone down the drain. I was surrounded by endings, and so it wasn't just my own end. But in a way, the crisis also helped: there was something new in this state of affairs, something powerful that demanded us to rethink ourselves and our idea of happiness. Which pushed us to sow new seeds, rename adopted plants. Seeding and renaming our concepts of family, hope, corpses in pots. Being in an individual state of crisis in the middle of a general state of crisis seemed better to me than being in a state of crisis in the middle of a lack of it.

'Do you want to hang?' my friends took turns in asking.

'Will you manage to be with me, even in our distance?' my new boyfriend asked.

I came up with excuses as to why I couldn't get myself organised. I preferred to be alone, or alone with Nico. That was the only thing that made me happy: my flat, our distance, the two of us alone. And this surprised me, because over the past few years I had felt constricted, shut in the house with a small child and a husband when all I'd wanted to do was run away. Often, I'd done it: I had run away. Now, though, I wanted to stay. Start repotting myself. But in this new place, I couldn't write: I no longer recognised my people or my hands, and I had to relearn everything afresh. Relearn to say I love you, for instance. And even the letter A. A.

The Sea Belonged to Us Too

Around that time, an Indian businessman had contacted my mother, with a mind to purchasing the Roland Ultra. This Indian gentleman's job entailed purchasing second-hand printing machines to ship back to his country. He looked for them on the internet, which was how he had found my mother's art gallery, when a Google Images search had brought up a photograph of the machine housed in the middle of the largest of the exhibition rooms.

In its heyday, the Roland Ultra had been a glorious, expensive machine. It had been used to print prestigious illustrated art books and encyclopaedias. The same books my grandfather had placed in my hands whenever I had visited him. Now the Roland Ultra was no longer used to print books, but it often featured in artists' performances: slowly, it had become something of a monument to what the press used to be. Some artists had used it for the sounds it made, others to print large-scale posters, or as a stage to perform on.

Me, I'd been hosting a literary festival named after my grandfather's printing machine, where authors were invited to sit on the Roland Ultra to talk about their lives. From time to time, the Roland Ultra sent out an electric shock and so the authors perched precariously on top of it, talking about their mothers and their habits in candlelight, taking care not to disturb the machine. Occasionally, an author had even been mildly electrocuted by those decade-old cogs – just a gentle shock that made the audience laugh – though the authors themselves tended to be markedly less amused.

My mother, who is a kind and educated soul, listened to what the Indian gentleman had to say until he had finished, then she rejected his proposal.

'The machine's not for sale,' she said.

Then she told him about my grandfather, about the press and how the Roland Ultra had become a monument to those rooms. He listened to my mother attentively, as if he were trying to figure out the ramifications of her words, and all of their hidden meanings. Then he thanked her and asked her to think about his offer a little longer. My mother said she would think about it, but she was still pretty sure she didn't want to sell the Roland Ultra.

'In India, your machine would print again,' the Indian man said. 'Here, it can't do that anymore.'

They said goodbye, wishing each other the best of luck.

Meanwhile, my father had gone bankrupt because of the financial crisis and other separate matters and had been forced to close down his office. My brother Teo, who worked for him, had not been paid for several months, and eventually received a severance payment in the region of a thousand euros. They'd come up with something new together, just the two of them, while the rest of the staff had had to be sent home. I wondered how my brother would cope, raising a young daughter on such little money. I earned more than he did, and it still wasn't easy for me. I wondered what it felt like to be in the middle of a crisis for him, and for my father, and other fathers, and sons, out there in the world.

When I was a little girl, my father's office used to take up two whole floors and employ many people. He'd opened his publishing house with my mother. When they'd first started, they'd lived on the premises, in a single room, with my sister Allegra. Later, when things had started going well and the company expanded, they'd moved into new houses and took up roomier offices. They'd worked all the time, so we'd barely ever crossed paths with them at home. My mother hadn't breastfed us, nor raised us in any conventional sense: as soon as we'd reached two months old, she'd gone back to working full time. They'd become very wealthy by devising and publishing many successful books and magazines and bought their family a very large home. We had a garden. We had trees, tortoises, wild strawberries. My mother and father never took us to school, nor did they pick us up; they didn't take us swimming or to ballet lessons. We had people for that who lived with us and were paid to do such things. We had a driver, English nannies and a cook. Skiing weekends and most of the other holidays were arranged in the same way. Then things had started to go wrong, they'd broken up and, almost simultaneously, their office space was cut back to a floor and a half. Then a single floor. Towards the end, the publishing house only took up half a floor, and all the rooms looked empty anyway. They were looking for other tenants to split the expenses.

As a little girl, I'd been very happy to have a rich mother and a rich father. I was happy that they were rich because they worked with books and magazines. Theirs was a guiltless wealth, it seemed to me, because it had been amassed through creativity and culture. Visiting the publishing house was an electrifying experience: something interesting was always going on in each of the rooms. Someone was working on the layout for a magazine, someone else was on the phone, or laughing, telling an anecdote, arguing. I was very happy with the publishing house, its audiobooks and the women's quarterlies, the guidebooks and VHS tapes. Us kids went to the Montessori school, where we learnt how to have faith in ourselves and be free, and our family could afford this luxury, even though there were four of us. Each morning, at the Montessori school, we were free to choose what we wanted to do, the only rule was to complete our work by the end of the day and in an orderly fashion. We took summer classes in England and winter breaks in Switzerland, where we owned a house. We were able to attend ballet classes, theatre classes, horse-riding and tennis lessons; we had everything we needed and much, much more.

During the years we still lived at home, tending to our liberal arts studies, we were also entitled to eat in whatever way suited us best. Vegetarian, pescatarian, slimming diets were all catered for. As teenagers we studied with famous dancers, artists, actors and film directors, all over the world. Some of us found spiritual guides to follow in lengthy meditation seminars, went to India to study yoga, or Belgium to learn dressage. Our mother took us to all the museums in New York, London, Copenhagen, to see whatever we should and wanted to see. My father rarely joined us on these trips, and I wondered whether he was keeping lovers. If he did turn up, he'd find a way to leave quickly afterwards and, again, I would think of his lovers. We didn't believe he liked being part of our family very much. For years, we owned a house in St Barth. A house in Paris. There was a house in Brazil we never even visited once. We travelled everywhere in the world, buying, choosing. Hawaii, China. We sailed to the Côte d'Azur, the Balearics, Greece or the Caribbean in our family boat. The sailboat was named after me and my older sister, the speedboat after our younger brother and sister.

We had many clothes, toys and a room full of VHS tapes with films that hadn't been released in cinemas yet. So we watched a lot of films: sometimes my sisters and I would watch two or three in a row, and no one would find out, because the house had several floors and it was easy to hide in there, to lose sight of one another. For instance, two floors separated my bedroom from that of my parents. Watching *Scenes from a Marriage* at age ten hadn't been a particularly wise idea, nor had *Fanny and Alexander*, a film that took over our nights and our dreams. At lunch and at dinner we were served individually, by the maid and the waiter, dressed in full uniform and gloves. The handsome gardener visited regularly, with his handsome assistants. There was a lot of money, many objects, too many computers, various phone lines to call from one room to another, a lift to move across the different floors, and lots of everything else. We studied what we had to study: languages, art, musical instruments, sports. We read a lot of books. We were politically active and participated in demonstrations, occupations, gatherings in social centres where we discussed philosophical and theological texts. We filled up charity bags for refugees and all sorts of displaced people, but there was definitely too much money around for us not to sense what role it might have.

I wasn't sad that my father was now poorer. Only, I worried that being poor might make him sad, and complicate my brother's life.

'How's it going, Dad?' I asked him one night. 'Are you worried?'

I don't remember where I was calling him from; he was at home.

We spoke two or three times a year. On a good year, four. Of him – of our life together – I carry with me the memory of a few nights spent discussing history or philosophy, laughing and playing and fighting with my siblings, and the time he beat me when I was seven because I'd slammed a door, and gave me a black eye that lasted for about a month. He'd beaten me and immediately I lied to my schoolmates, my teachers and my grandfather, coming up with a story that meant it wasn't his fault. I also carry the memory of a night when I had an ear infection, and he kept his hand on my ear until dawn, to heal me and so I wouldn't be afraid. I carry his silences and his idiosyncrasies, and the time he slapped my big sister, and they were shouting you piece of shit to each another, and the memory of yet another night he must have smoked a spliff, because he had a panic attack and had to be taken to hospital by my mother. I carry the things I think I know about him: his betrayals, his big brain, his strange heart and his many injustices against my mother. The grave illness that struck him down as a child, his terrible boarding school, his all-resistant solitude in the face of the world. And so he'd been born a commoner. Grew up rich as his parents got rich. Became poor by choice when he'd chosen to become a communist and a waiter, and then rich again thanks to his own hard work. Now he was poor, despite his hard work, and he certainly no longer considered himself a communist. Above all, he was poor in a new phase of his life: his sixties.

'I'm dandy. I'm not worried.'

'What will you do now?'

'I've thirty cardboard boxes sitting in front of me, and I'm not sure what I will do with them. They're full of all my favourite books. It seems perfect,' he told me, in a jolly mood.

'Are you going to have to leave the flat?'

'It's a possibility.'

'Where will you go?'

'I don't know that yet.'

He sounded as if he were at peace. Once, I'd been commissioned to write an article on happiness for a magazine. 'What's your idea of happiness?' I'd asked my father by email that evening. He'd answered that his idea of happiness was being locked in a prison or monastery, so he could finally think in some depth. It wasn't that I'd believed him, but that I worried he might believe it himself. That he still felt the need to say this kind of thing, which typically turned out to be meaningless, in the end.

'Interesting times,' he said on the phone. 'Everything new, everything to be reimagined.'

We talked about other things. My life, Nico. The work trips I needed to take. His new girlfriend, with whom he did not share a flat. I figured it didn't matter whether he was actually worried and whether the times he was living through weren't actually that interesting, because he had chosen to say so to me, and I had no reason to force him to claim the opposite. My father seemed to believe what he'd told me, at least with a part of himself, and I had to admire the detached way in which he dealt with pain, endings and crisis.

'Has Maria been coming round to look after your plants?' he asked me. 'The trees on my balcony are sick. Can you send me her number?'

'All right, but I can't guarantee she will come, because I don't think she's going back to work properly yet. Aren't you moving anyway?'

'I guess so,' he concluded. Which didn't change things: plants need looking after, even while moving.

I spoke to him again a few days later. He told me that the kid who'd been helping him out with the move had mistakenly tossed out the boxes of books to be kept instead of the ones to be taken to the recycling centre.

'How are you coping?' I asked.

'Interesting times,' he said.

We hung up and fell out of touch again. I'm not used to his presence, so once more, I forgot him immediately. I never miss my father: he never wanted me to miss him, and I've long adjusted to that.

'It's useless to pretend you don't care. It's not true,' the psychic says.

'Pretend I don't care about what?' I try. My father, the priests at his boarding school, my grandfather, my new boyfriend, my husband, my son: all the men in my world are laughing. They're looking at me. I'm looking at them.

'All right, then,' the psychic says.

Meanwhile, my new old book had been published, and every time I did an event someone in the audience would start crying. I kept having fits overnight, during which I was seized by a terrible stomach-ache. Sometimes I passed out. It was very Fanny Ardant in *The Woman Next Door*, when Depardieu kisses her and she passes out with too much love, too much feeling.

That book, in a way, was still painful for me, too alive. I'd taken inspiration from my own love, and as I punched the walls at night, I told myself that this kind of pain was similar to giving birth. Very Ardant of me, again. But giving birth had been beautiful as well, while this pain didn't seem to be useful for anything. The following day, the pain would be gone, and I'd feel better. Then a little better each day. It bothered me that people thought I was suffering because of the end of my love, and so I'd always switch the subject. I'd been following a rigid diet, maybe it was that, I said. I'd been working too much, perhaps that had contributed to my current state? I was happy, too, because I'd just fallen in love again. And I was already in love in a way from before, in love with the old idea of us – my husband and me – and so I had dreams about my husband still, wondering whether we could ever go back. Nonetheless, something in those dreams was coming to an end. I was simultaneously nostalgic for the past and hungry for the future before me. I kept going back to the moments I had lived – our letters, photographs, memories – while I created new ones – new letters, new photographs, new memories of a new love to learn and preserve. My bag kept filling up with plane tickets to Britain. My new love was taking up space, becoming my new landscape, my new land. Plus, at home, there were all those plants to look after, all those holes from which Nico needed protecting.

'What are you going to wear for the divorce?' I asked my mother.

'I haven't thought about that.'

'And the truth is?'

'I bought a dress,' she admitted.

I spoke to her again the day after the divorce. I spoke to her in kind tones, she answered back in kind.

'How was it?'

'Sad. But also nice. We went for lunch after.'

'Did you make love?' I asked her.

'No,' she said, curtly. 'We're very different women, you and I.'

Months later my mother confessed she'd also thought about making love to him after they'd signed the divorce papers. But it was true, still: we were very different women, she and I. And me and my sister Diana. And Maria and me. And all our endings were different, yet it was impossible not to think of them as connected, not to think about them as unexceptional, individually, and none of them really an ending but part of an interconnected, continuous movement in which, when one of the elements came to rest, another continued its trajectory.

I kept finding proof of my feeling that everything was collapsing and changing. Could the crash of Apple's stocks have anything to do with us? Could we have anything to do with the euro crisis, Egypt and the jellyfish invasion that had violently returned to our seas? How to deal with all those jellyfish was a thought that kept me up at night. Would we have to explain to our children how, once upon a time, we'd been able to dive into the sea, that the sea had once belonged to us too? How would we cope when we'd no longer be able to fish in the Mediterranean Sea?

Earth was collapsing and we kept running in circles, trying to keep in step. And even in my pain and in my fear, I felt excited calculating the sum of our disasters, and finding they added up, after all, to possibility. We were in the same year that the end of the world had been predicted to happen, and I'd become attached to those premonitions that pictured our final demise. If everything was ending, what was it even, an end? The word lost its meaning. I kept running in circles, my tongue hanging out, and I always felt thirsty.

'I've bought lots of bottled water and tinned food to prepare for the end of the world,' my sister Allegra told me on the phone, calling from the other end of the world.

'To save yourself?' I asked.

'To save you too.'

'I wouldn't know how to get there: they say it won't be about food or water. We'll leave from our front door – if we'll still have a house and a front door – and right on our doorstep: the desert. A desert! Ha! What am I saying. A postapocalyptic, moonlike landscape, with no directions or coordinates. We won't even be able to say "desert" or "help me".'

'I've got water,' my sister repeated, 'chickpeas and rice. You should try to join me.' That my only safe haven and my only allocated chickpea tin were both in New Zealand made my chances for survival appear rather thin.

Branches and Soil Everywhere

Maria had called to say it wasn't going to rain the following day, and so she would come to see me.

'I hope we'll get in the habit of making plans depending on the rain, rather than our other engagements,' I told her.

'How else should we make plans?' she asked.

I got the door for her while I was on the phone, and she smiled at me. She began carrying up tools and bags of soil from the courtyard. Nursery pots and gloves, shears and packs of fertiliser. I worried about her blood and her brain. I imagined the excessive strain of all that carrying. Was she pushing herself too hard? If I felt worried about her, did that mean that something bad was about to happen? Was I now destined to be Maria's saviour forever, due to some unforeseen magic power?

'Do you need help?' I asked her.

She shook her head and disappeared again. She settled herself on the terrace and began breaking old earth and pulling out dried roots, snapping dead branches. I watched her get to work, and as she did, I began writing. I had a deadline looming, and many emails I needed to answer.

So she worked as I worked. She, close to the plants, while her hair grew back on her head, and me, on my keyboard, with fresh new pages piling up beside me. After a couple hours, I went out to see her. There were branches and soil everywhere. She was sweating as she bent over and pulled. It was an ugly terrace: dirty, bare and ugly. With bags of soil everywhere, and so much in need of help. My plants were all dried out. Black holes. Old pots. Broken vessels.

'We've got rid of everything dry, broken or dead. Anything that's left in an acceptable condition, we'll keep. This is the time to cut back. Don't be scared seeing it this way.'

I listened without comment. I took stock of the deaths and arranged for the disposal of the bodies. Each of Maria's words seemed to me like a metaphor that needed deciphering: thinking about her sentences this way, as if they offered a sentimental or existential translation of lived experience, made me want to laugh. Don't be scared seeing it this way! Let's keep anything left that's acceptable!

'This pot's broken. That one needs changing. That pot is plastic, that's cement, this is terracotta.'

I hadn't realised that. Had I never touched these pots before?

I kept listening to her, as a gust of wind lifted some branches, then a little soil. My stomach contracted: winter was everywhere. I had felt it so clearly a moment before, in that precise gust of air. After the wind passed, the future disappeared, and it was still autumn. Here was the present, but it was a new one.

'Are you hungry?' I asked Maria.

'Yeah,' she said.

I left her to work and went to make rice and a vegetable soup. I warmed up some tea. I cut the bread and set the table properly. When we sat down, a transparent, pure light filtered in from the windows.

'Thank you,' she said, before she began eating.

I almost never cooked during the day, and so I felt happy about this hot food and sitting at the table opposite Maria, and not my computer. I was happy that the vegetables had kept their crunch, and that both of us were alive. Maria always appeared to have lots of time and lots of patience. I always looked like I was in a hurry, chasing something.

'How did he replace you?' I asked her.

'You mean emotionally?'

'I mean, how did you find out.'

'Our house was always messy. He's usually a very tidy man.'

Maria was angry; you could tell that she still loved him. We polished off the soup, and I poured out seconds. We finished the first cup of tea and started on a fresh brew.

'It was like I didn't interest him anymore. And, truly, I wasn't as interesting as I used to be. I was tiresome and scared – just different. My body was different. But what else could I do?'

We finished our tea, and I cleared the table, gesturing to her that I didn't need help.

'Was he good to you while you were in hospital?' I asked.

'Really good.'

Maria was distraught. She explained that it's easier to tend to a suffering body than a recovering mind. You can't see the blood. Depression and fatigue are a pain to everyone else. We went back to the terrace. Maria was healthy, strong. I wondered if she was the kind of person who feels better by talking ill of their ex-partners after a break-up, or the kind of person who feels better remembering the good times.

'What makes you feel better, saying good or bad things about your ex-boyfriend?' I asked her.

'A bit of both,' she said. Sad forehead; happy mouth.

Later, I went to pick up Nico. We went back to the flat for a few minutes: I wanted to show him the terrace, where we were rebuilding life from the soil – the dry branches, the dead plants. I wanted to show him our present, including the dead branches that we needed to dispose of. Maria explained what she was doing, and Nico ate his afternoon snack while he watched her work. We said goodbye to her before leaving.

'If we're not back by the time you are finished, just leave the door on the latch,' I told Maria.

Nico kissed Maria on the cheek, and that day, as I walked in the street with my little boy, I felt very proud of myself. On the one hand because I am proud, generally, of being a mother, but above all because I am proud of being Nico's. In our new neighbourhood we often run into friends, other parents and other children, and shopkeepers, teachers of drama, swimming, English and gym classes. And in this new place – both emotionally and geographically – I am often moved to tears. I am moved to tears thinking that someone specifically decided to teach swimming, make bread or fix motorbikes. As in a game from when we were kids: you're the doctor, I'm the teacher and so on and so forth, only that it lasts a whole lifetime. Whenever I'm walking around here, seeing people I know, I can't stop thinking about us all cohabiting in the same neighbourhood, in this particular city, in this same world and over these same years, like extras on a film set, or characters in a novel taking place right here, in these few streets, in this time, almost exclusively ours. I think about our love. And our pain. I do, especially, when I go to my usual bar, and within a few moments of arriving, my husband comes in. It is the same bar I take my new boyfriend when he is in Milan. Typically, my husband will turn up with his girlfriend an hour or so later. Maybe we even use the same coffee cup, or the same coffee spoons, rinsed quickly under the steaming faucet. The staff here know everything about us and about everyone else: they're a running commentary on our lives, our Greek chorus. Sometimes my husband and I deliberately make plans to meet there, so we can drink a coffee in those very same cups, catching up about Nico and our respective lives. In that same bar, my husband and my boyfriend shook hands for the very first time. It is the very same bar in which I first saw my husband's new girlfriend from afar.

'She's a friend of mine,' he said, walking up to Nico and me.

'So why isn't she getting up to say hi?' I asked.

I also saw one of the mothers from Nico's school I'd seen crying by the public pool. I've spied on the arguments of couples I know, admired the barman kissing a girl in secret.

For each one of us I imagine a line made in red, blue or green pen, running alongside our feet on the ground. Our pathways, every step, the traces we have left behind in our lives: these appear to us as extraordinary journeys, maybe because they are sketched out in red, yet they've all been written out with a simple biro pen. Our flats are a single, huge home.

'What are you thinking about?' I ask Nico, as we walk.

'I'm not thinking,' he says.

'What are you doing, then?'

'I'm here with you. We're walking.'

When we get back to the flat, we find the door on the latch and a small jar of leaves and grass in the middle of the kitchen table. There are some small sprigs in it: mint. Next to it there's a note that says, 'I'm off, see you.' This is how I learn that you can put together a nice decorative green bunch without flowers. Without the need to purposefully cut, without a need for spring. All you need are some leaves, an ear of grain, greenery. What's left over from cutting is enough to put together something delicate but lovely: the neighbour's old plants can start a forest, the leftovers of a family are enough to survive in the desert.

'Teucrium', Maria has written on her note. We'll have something to look at, even in winter, and, in a way, something to celebrate. Our plants are ready to give us all that, always.

'You're breathing more easily,' the psychic says.

'Do you have a bigger pink quartz, by any chance?' I ask. She sits on my lap.

'You're speaking in the present tense,' she says.

'In the present or in the past?' I ask.

'Everywhere,' she says. 'You're present everywhere, and to us all. Keep at it!'

what's left over from cutting

Meanwhile, Diana is looking for a new place. I watch it all happen as if I am standing on a very high terrace: moving boxes and vans, walls being painted, furniture shifted. From up here, I have a clear view, welcoming only what's necessary. The movement is unstoppable, fluid, continuous. A beastly traffic of moving kilograms and kilometres. Large parking lots. Packing tape noise on brown cardboard. Marker pens scrawling on boxes: kitchen, bedroom, my books, your books. Signs hanging on buildings, announcing: 'Moving today'. New lives. Dreams. My husband and I leaving our shared home. More boxes.

Vans. My husband leaving his new home shortly after he moved in, to move into his new new home. Boxes. More vans. My sister finding a new home for herself. Boxes. Vans. My grandfather's bedframe being delivered to me. Maria leaving her boyfriend's place. My grandmother leaving the home she had lived in forever. My father his office. Boxes. Vans. Boxes. Vans. Each of the flats we move into had to be emptied beforehand. Every project altered, re-thought, re-chosen, abandoned. The former tenant of my current flat moving away. Boxes. Vans. Her husband moving out of the flat I now live in, a few months before she did. Boxes. Vans. Our movement is heart-rending and absurd, simultaneously useless. It hurts and at the same time feels like nothing at all.

'How do you want your new house to look?' I ask my sister Diana.

'Either very big, so I could let out a room, or very small, so that I'm able to afford it by myself.'

'You're looking for two completely opposite things at the same time.'

'So are you,' she laughs. 'And quite likely everyone else.'

Happy with her eyes. Sad with her mouth.

Over the past few months, in the throes of this emotional and practical frenzy, I have convinced myself that I will never go back to writing. I wonder how I'll be able to let go of another dream that belonged to my life before the crisis, and how I'll adjust it to my new circumstances, along with all the other dreams I've had to adjust. It has everything to do with giving up on something complex, such as the very meaning of the person one thought they were. Will books still exist in the future, anyway? And why write if all things on Earth, its history and nature, are disappearing? How to focus on anything else but jellyfish and every moment of Nico's life? I try not to think about it, to pretend I'm still the same person even though everything around me is different, but for some reason I've grown attached to the idea that my previous routine was the right one for me to be able to write. My husband. Our old house. Nico, but younger – or before Nico was born altogether. My unhappiness and my happiness with them. I begin writing two new possible books, nevertheless, to demonstrate I can still be diligent. Sixty pages into the first, I abandon my protagonists suspended in a cable car hanging over a precipice, and they never come down again. It takes me ninety pages to accept that I won't finish the second either. When I abandon my protagonists, they are running away from a park in the city of London. One of the kids has stabbed another, and I have no stamina to rescue any of them.

'Are you writing?' my mother asks me again.

'It's all I do,' I say.

'Don't be such a socialite, then.'

'I'm always home actually.'

'Definitely less than Virginia Woolf,' she says.

I pretend my own opinion differs from hers, when I am actually in agreement. I'm not a socialite, but everything distracts me. Shared cups in cafes. Dogs. Biro pen lines. My own thoughts, in which I keep coming up guilty. I don't love people enough. I don't look after people when they are suffering. I didn't call Maria when she was in hospital. I didn't call Alessandro when he was in hospital. I didn't make my son a little brother or sister. I didn't hug my husband enough. I cheated. My plants are half dead. I don't visit my grandmother often enough. When my grandfather died, I wasn't much help to her. I wasn't much help to my mother either. I've never managed to sort things out with my father. I don't allow my new love to become the love it could be. In my dreams, I commit murder and I'm never punished for it.

'How are you, Grandma?' I call her.

'Really well. I went on a really nice walk today. Then I played cards. Now I've a friend over for tea. How's your little boy?'

My grandmother is happy. Sometimes she says she's got the 'anguishes' – it's always 'anguishes', in the plural – but she says so while smiling. Saying 'anguishes', in the plural, makes it seem less threatening. Anguish, of the senseless kind – the fear of death – only exists in the singular. When my grandmother has the flu, she says she is ready to die, but when the flu passes, she's definitely not ready to die.

'Nico is sweet, kind,' I say.

'When are you bringing him to see me?'

'Maybe tomorrow. I'll let you know if I can fit it in.'

'Sure, but don't worry about it,' my grandmother reassures me.

'I'll try.'

'And what about my plants?' she asks.

'Maria came. She's looking after them. They're getting used to the new place.'

My grandmother doesn't want us grandchildren to

trouble ourselves about her, to worry about her or cross the city to visit her. That's not true, in fact. I know she is desperate to see me, but above all she is desperate not to cause a fuss. I already know I won't fit in a visit tomorrow. I know that full well. I wish I could see her all the time, and I barely ever do see her. I wish she would never die, and I don't want to die either. I'm desperate not to die. When she found out I was divorcing my husband, my grandmother commented with a single sentence:

'Oh well. What are you gonna do about that.'

Oh well. What am I gonna do about that.

In the evenings, Nico and I sit on the terrace before the sun sets. It's cold and so we put on our coats and scarves. We often leave our shoes inside. Sometimes a blackbird comes near, but it never lands on the terrace. When one of us points it out to the other, it has already flown away. We've never seen the blackbird together in the same moment. But we do talk about it, a lot. The blackbird looks like this, the blackbird does that.

The blackbird looks like this,
The blackbird does that

'In a month or two we'll be able to eat outside,' I tell him.

'How long is a month?' Nico asks.

I'm not sure how to explain how long a month is. We stare at our new piece of sky and with our frozen feet we measure our new square metres of space. We measure out the time in which we're alone together, waiting for nobody to come back home. Silence and time. I rearrange my fears and learn to recognise a new emotion, which fills up my heart from time to time much like a panic attack, but which is in turn an attack of happiness. It is a kind of happiness that is always close to the brink of tears, as if I am experiencing romantic delirium.

Out on the terrace, Nico enjoys grabbing the soil from the pots, until I tell him it is forbidden, because the plants could die. I'm not even sure if this is true, but I don't want him to cause a mess, unsettling the plants and their roots. We survey all of them, one by one, every day. I've still not learnt their names, except for the easy ones: rose and mint. Little else.

'They don't change much in winter,' I explain.

'Why?'

'They're more or less asleep. They're quiet.'

He likes looking at the plants, and so do I. He wishes for an apricot tree. He wishes for a puppy. He wishes that birds would land on his shoulder. He asks me how to plant broccoli. He hangs out on his skateboard or his scooter, while I spy on the windows of others, their lights coming on and going off: other families, houses, nearby and far. I imagine a collective world meeting in which we will all hug and reassure each other that everything will be OK. I imagine a huge family in which everyone is capable of laughing and loving. A huge bed full of children. My grandfather's bed full of children. Sometimes, my grandfather's bed full of a father, a mother and many children. If I'm in a good mood, I stick my grandmother and a few of her friends in there. I smell out the plants of the city and as I breathe in it's like I'm taking in all the plants in the world, connecting them all to the same irrigation system. I stay like this – we both stay – wrapped up in my scarf, checking that Nico is wrapped up warm enough, because his throat gets cold when my throat gets cold, and my throat gets cold when the same happens to his. Is that how everyone's throats in the world work?

'Come to me,' my new boyfriend tells me. I say yes more often now; pack my bags. I go through the necessary check-ins and board planes.

'You're changing shape,' the psychic whispers.

'Is that mandatory?' I ask.

'If you'd rather, we can just have a coffee,' she smiles. 'But I'm telling you, I make famously terrible coffee.'

I'm beginning to choke. She's still sitting on my legs, squeezing me. I squeeze her back. The pink quartz falls to the floor. It doesn't break, but I'm worried the psychic is angry. I look closely at her face: she's not angry. She lifts the quartz and places it between us once again. I look at my hands, I open them and find a flower.

'Eat it,' the psychic says. And I eat the flower in a heartbeat.

So Green, So Resilient

So, while Maria broke up with her boyfriend and I flew back and forth over the Alps to see mine, while Diana and Alessandro broke up too, Alessandro met Luisa again. Luisa was his girlfriend from many centuries earlier. She'd come to see how he was coping with his novel near-death experience. As he recovered, they fell in love again, and got back together.

'It's an odd thing to say, but the accident, in a way, was the best thing that could ever have happened to me,' Alessandro explains. 'It brought me Luisa, and it made me change. I'd been feeling unlucky and lonely. But so many people looked after me. I had to take a forced break, and that forced me in turn to take care of myself and understand who I really am. I am certain I've made people suffer. My mother has a whole new face these days – she's piled on the years. Still, I am happy this happened to me.'

When he tells me this I burst into tears, and so does he. We all cry very often, that's for sure. Finally, it rains often these days. I look at one of Alessandro's hospital papers, which I have asked him to bring. At the top it says: 'Type of accident: frontal collision, motorbike'.

'I used to tell myself that nobody loved me. But I had to change my mind after the accident.'

By chance, we happen to be in the same restaurant where my mother and father had lunch after signing the divorce papers. I tell Alessandro. He understands.

'Well, the girl who just came through the door is the girl I was drinking with on the night of the accident,' he retaliates, smiling.

'If I may add: on the day of the accident, Maria and I were talking about you while we were standing next to the Roland Ultra. So perhaps it is meaningful also to mention that the machine is about to be shipped to India, where it'll go back to printing again.'

As I tell him about the Roland Ultra, I'm thinking about the people who'd come to visit me in hospital, if I had an accident. My husband, or my new boyfriend? I look at Alessandro and we order another coffee. He and Diana still see each other sometimes. They're nearly friends. They're able to go out to dinner and have a chat. They're also able to argue or cry, just as we all seem to like doing. Sometimes Diana tells me she's upset that Alessandro is seeing somebody else. Other times she feels perfectly fine about it and not at all upset. I don't know if she's aware of how much she can shift from one mood to its opposite, but I suspect what she says is all she can say, because it is all she believes in, each time. Get away from me. Come closer. You're the reason I'm alive. I'm only alive when I'm away from you.

So, the Roland Ultra is about to leave for India. It is true that my mother had never thought of selling it before, but when the Indian gentleman suggested it, she immediately began to consider the possibility. Primarily, I think, because of her long history with India: for quite some time, my mother has wished she were Indian in her previous life. Sometimes she shows us the photographs of Indian children or entire Indian families who have offered to adopt her during her trips. She's taken many photographs of Indian cows and Indian cow shit lined up on the banks of the River Ganges. It follows, then, that an Indian gentleman seeking to obtain the Roland Ultra is a different matter than, for instance, an Italian gentleman. She would have taken the least pleasure in an Englishman. My mother doesn't much like people in London; they are too materialistic; they are too rich. Now that I spend part of my time there, she likes London even less.

'It's a city for socialites,' she keeps saying. 'Just like you.'

'You know, in London I'm staying near the first house Virginia Woolf lived in,' I try.

In second place, my mother might have capitulated to a Frenchman, instead of an Indian, and sold him the Roland Ultra, because she's always wished she could live in Paris, and French people, she feels, behave in appropriately seductive ways towards her. Anyway, all the other machines from my grandfather's printing press had been sold over time. Only the Roland Ultra remained, because it was beautiful and strong, and we had all grown so attached to it. When my mother asked our opinion, I didn't like the idea of it leaving.

'It's the spirit of the place,' I said. 'It shouldn't leave. Without it, all that's left is three big empty rooms.'

'But in India it would go back to printing again,' she said in an Indian accent, to make me laugh.

'How much are they paying?' I asked, forcing myself not to laugh at her Indian accent.

'It's not about the money,' she said. 'Anyway: ten grand.'

'I don't want you to sell,' I said.

When my grandfather had bought it, the Roland Ultra had been worth a billion lire. It was a sum I had only seen written in comic books as a child. One billion! We'd had to change our understanding of the word 'billion' since. Imagine winning a billion at the lottery! The Indian gentleman who wanted to buy the machine had a printing press, which he'd converted into a hospital for the needy. What chance did I have against so much justice? So much justice bundled up inside a singular Indian man? At a dinner party, my mother spoke about the Roland Ultra's potential departure to an artist friend. He said it seemed like a beautiful journey and encouraged her to follow the machine to its destination herself.

'I don't want you to sell,' I repeated. But no one was listening to me.

On the day they begin to dismantle the machine, my grandfather's former employees come to say goodbye to it. Some artists swing by to take pictures or sketch it one final time. Once the first part of the cover is removed, its bolts and a large pipe inside make the machine look even more like an elephant, currently undergoing surgery. Hidden in the Roland are small, round engines, delicately fitted. It's cold, and the pictures from that morning tell a story from the depths of winter. When I finally meet Mr Bharat, he tells me that it took a whole day to dismantle the Roland, but it will take an entire month to put it back together once it reaches its destination. 'It takes no time to destroy, it is very long to create,' he explains. The parts of the Roland are loaded on trucks and then into containers, in which they will cross the sea until they reach India; meanwhile, where we are, the days are becoming shorter, and half of the right side of my terrace has been colonised by mint.

The mint on my terrace smells lovely but is very invasive. It's taken up space between the roots and the leaves of the other plants. I use it for cooking, and in the morning when the sun's out – even if it's only a cold winter sun – the mint sends out a potent smell similar to that of marijuana. It isn't a particularly good variety of mint to eat, so sometimes, when I make sautéed courgettes or lentils with it, it spoils the whole dish. It can leave a bitter, unpredictable aftertaste in your mouth: after all, the person who planted it was sad from the nose up, and happy from the nose down.

Before I had a terrace with mint growing on it, I had no idea so many varieties of it even existed. When somebody comes to visit, I cut off some branches and wrap them in newspaper for them to take home as a gift. I make mint tea. I tear out its leaves for Nico to smell. I warn everyone that sometimes the mint tastes good, sometimes bad. In any case, we're enjoying an inexhaustible, free edible treat.

'We've got to get this mint under control,' Maria has been saying from the beginning.

I nod, but in truth I have no clue about how to control a mint plant. Maria knows things about the future that are obscure to me. She can foretell how a plant will grow, for instance, while I still find it all a surprise. Maria knows that, though the mint seems tame now, looking quite spare, one day it will grow thick and excessive. I thought that was a sign of healthy growth: growing everywhere, excessively. My mint even grows in the fissures between the tiles and on the terrace ledge. I don't know how to prune a plant to make it grow less. I don't know how to limit infestation or how to live in this new flat. I don't know how to let go of the Roland Ultra, so it may print again, nor how to deal with all this change.

'Do you want some mint?' I keep asking everybody, because it seems to me the only kind way I have of getting rid of it gently.

My mother's mint always tastes nice. She has much less of it, which she keeps in good order. It's tasty.

'Can I have some mint?' I ask when I go over to see her.

But my mother only keeps a little mint at her place: it's under control, so she rarely has any to give away. Sure, mine's invasive, but it's also beautiful to look at. So green, so resilient.

Maybe because of the mint, the terrace or the silence, Nico and I have started to feel better living here, and this is also thanks to the fact that we have kind neighbours. We see these kind neighbours often, as they also look after their plants, spending time in the open air as we do. I never saw anyone when I lived in any of my previous houses. My neighbours are better than me at looking after their plants: peppers, aubergines and flowers populate their balconies and the outdoor walkways of the condominium that we share. They keep succulents, olive trees and flowering plants. Whenever I bump into my neighbours, I want to alert them to the fact that, after a slow start, I've now begun looking after the plants on my balcony and on the upstairs terrace, and that soon, with Maria's help, they will do better. I want to explain that I needed to settle in first before I could do that. But all I seem to be able to say is hello. I smile, I say hello, and little else.

Slowly, though, I begin to linger, petting their dogs and cats. We'll become friends, I tell myself, once Nico and I manage to convince birds to land on our shoulders and help us make the bed, lay the table and dance.

Then in the evening, when I am scared of the noises and the darkness, I think about the old wooden doors of our flat and their faltering locks. Just a strong shove and they would collapse, so if I'm feeling in danger, I repeat to myself that I have kind neighbours. Families, children, couples and pets. There's a cat only a few centimetres away from me. An olive tree. A small dog opposite. A mother. They're separated from Nico and me by a wall, but we're certainly on the same side. For sure we'd all fit in my grandfather's bed. I know we're not a family, but at the same time I know we are one. I keep falling asleep with the light on, the way I used to before I moved in with my husband.

'I'm switching your light off,' I tell Nico, instead.

'Leave the door open,' he says. 'I'm scared.'

'There's nothing to be scared of,' I convince him.

'Could I be the first person who lives forever?' he asks.

'You could be,' I tell him. As I say it, I'm sure it could actually happen.

At his age, I, too, was afraid of the dark, and I already wanted the light on while I slept. Only now I understand how many of the things my mother told me to reassure me couldn't have been true for her either. Nothing bad will happen. I'm right here. It's nothing, Maria. Just a congestion. Maybe a touch of heatstroke. Mothers never get ill. Nor children. I will love you forever.

Sometimes, at night, my husband and I text.

How are you? I ask him. All's well here. Nico's asleep, I add in another text. Sometimes he replies at eleven the following morning.

Sorry, I was asleep. Or he says, All's well. Maybe I'll come round later.

Later when? I ask.

Access to my flat is both orderly and disorderly. Does he mean later, after school ends? Later, during dinner? Later in a metaphorical sense? Is he saying 'maybe' because he definitely *won't* make it, but a tentative phrasing sweetens the pill? Is he eating with us, or no? I'll text you after my lunch break. I'll see how I'm doing. Often, we communicate in this way, without making fixed plans or adding much else. If I'm in a good mood, I don't dwell on it. If I'm in a bad mood, I think about what the therapist told us: 'You must plan ahead. You can't have unfettered access to each other's house.' Now I understand what he meant about being vague, and how we could hurt one another that way. Distance has slowly complicated our habits. Our separate lives have taken up space, like my mint. He doesn't have to account for what he gets up to. My husband is not the man I should be waiting for. My home is not our home. We all fit in my grandfather's bed except for him. Sometimes, at night, I dream of cooking him dinner and he doesn't turn up. When, rarely, he does, he tells me the meat is too tough and I should stop eating differently, stop following my vegetarian diet. Sometimes I dream that he asks me to marry him.

'I love you,' I tell my new boyfriend.

'I've never been in love like this before,' he says.

'I love you so much,' I add.

I miss my boyfriend when he's not there, and in a way now, I'm missing everyone, always. By that I mean I am also missing the hugs and kisses of the seven billion people on Earth whom I've never met.

'You're here to love!' the psychic yells. 'There's nothing wrong with that! There's nothing wrong with resting.'

'You mean nesting?' I ask.

'Shut up, all right?' she says. She kisses me firmly on the mouth before shouting the word love in my face again.

I receive the kiss and the word love from her, while I try to remain motionless. It's a fake stillness, like that of the plants, which seem motionless while they spread everywhere, growing continuously, taking up ninety-nine point five per cent of our whole planet.

The Garden Is Ready to Rest

I receive an email from Maria in which she recaps everything she's been doing on the terrace over her past few visits: the hours she put in; our next immediate needs. I read her email over and over again, trying to memorise some of the plant names.

'If you give them a name, it means they exist!' I tell myself.

But the plants are so many, and their names seem to grow ever more complex. I receive another, more technical email. That, too, I memorise.

Anna,

I've taken the power boxes apart and put them to bed. I took the batteries out – they're in the bottom drawer of the red chest of drawers. I forgot to tell you: last time I planted some spring bulbs – I won't tell you where, you'll find out in due time. They'll be the first to come through.

I've wrapped up the lemon tree in muslin. It looks a little ghostly, but it'll have some protection should the cold get too harsh. Nico's bedroom warms up the terrace from below, but it's windy up there, so I'd rather not risk it. I've cleaned up and pruned what needed pruning: your garden is ready to rest. Not quite yet though. In a little while. Maria

I like how she's written 'I've taken the power boxes apart and put them to bed'. I like the names of the plants. Her practical life. I also like her price list, where her own manual work is included in Latin, under 'labour'. Now I know that my irrigation system stops working in winter, and that the electrical components must be taken apart, otherwise they'll freeze, and then the pipes will freeze. Everyone else probably already knew that – maybe even I did, like the word *labour*, or how to be a mother, even before I became one. But I'm noticing sounds, colours and words that I wasn't noticing before. Every person's fragility. Plant language, swarm language: our language. Aneurysms and weddings taking place in front of the Roland Ultra. My grandfather's Roland, now in India. The restaurant I meet Alessandro in, which is the same restaurant where my mother and father had lunch after signing the divorce papers. Used coffee cups, quickly rinsed out and used once again. By this point I'm obsessively looking for connections with anyone else who happens to inhabit the Earth at the same time as myself. I don't see anyone or anything individually, but only in movement, as connected to the rest. We are no longer people but one huge blurry stain, water in an irrigation system, blood in the veins, life happening, all at once.

'Did you ever notice that the Roland, which translates to Orlando in Italian, has the same name of the son of the first artist who included it in one of his pieces?' I tell my mother. 'Does he know that?'

'Know what?' my mother asks.

'The artist, Luca Pancrazzi. Does he know he named his own son after our machine?'

'Enough of these phoney connections, please,' she says.

My mother tells me this as we are on our way to the funeral of a close friend of hers. He was a special friend, one of a kind. We all loved him deeply. That day, in church, Maria returns the scarf she had kept from the day of her aneurysm. On the same day, magically early, my mother's rosebush, which her dead friend gave her, blossoms for the first time.

'There you go! *This* is a connection,' my mother says, looking at the roses. We smell them together.

It's very cold now and it gets dark early, so Nico and I are spending less time on the terrace. The plants need us less. I take the temperature of everything less often, with growing detachment. Am I unwell? Is Maria well, right at this moment? Are Alessandro's hands completely healed, or are they still healing, while simultaneously growing older and weaker? Should I jump on a plane, or can I stay here, where I am? We are ready to rest. We have cleaned out the dead things. Our roots are getting smarter.

'Come to me?' my new boyfriend asks.

'Come to us instead,' I say. 'We're taking turns from now on, all right?'

Because it's cold, Nico and I keep getting sick one after the other, and so sometimes we have to skip school or our other commitments. When I look at Nico, home sick from school, I recall the exact feeling of staying at home when I was little myself. The windowpanes separating me from the cold outside, during those precious, stolen hours at home, cartoons – half an hour of them, in the morning. Women's shows. My grandmother coming to visit. The adult world that existed without us, in the hours us children were usually away. Who would have suspected there was life in the places I didn't look at, and didn't inhabit?

My mother comes to visit us too. She's always liked looking after sick children in their pajamas. She brings a little gift for Nico, in the same way our grandmother always used to bring us a little gift: a fluorescent pen, a new notebook or stickers that smelt nice if you dragged your fingernail across them. I imagine myself as a grandmother. Bringing small gifts to my future grandchildren. I try to imagine having no teeth, running my tongue across my gums. I wonder how long before my mother loses hers. And what about me? Nico?

'It's too cold in this flat,' my mother tells me every time she comes to visit, and every time I feel the cold afresh, and my own home appears to me as more bare and uglier than it had seemed a minute before my mother arrived. She starts reading a small book to Nico, sneaking some almonds or a piece of chocolate from my kitchen cupboards. After barely an hour, she gets back on her bike and rides off. My mother likes to arrive here, but she almost prefers to leave. We also like it when she arrives, and we don't mind it when she goes away. I prefer Nico when he is alone with me, and he is softer and kinder.

'Stop telling Nico he's beautiful,' my mother tells me before she leaves.

'But he *is* beautiful!' I laugh.

'You don't say that to children!' she repeats, and she smiles, but it is also clear she really believes what she says. She really believes children shouldn't be told that they are beautiful, although I'm not sure why. Perhaps she's worried about Nico becoming too vain.

The few leaves left on my terrace become darker, and so does the city, and our piece of sky. We spend most of our time shut in the flat, because there aren't that many places outside we fancy visiting. Though there are only a few leaves on the floor, I still sweep the terrace every evening – sometimes earlier than that, now it's already dark by 5 p.m.

My husband comes round for dinner less often, and once Nico starts spending the night over at his, I also visit them less. To begin with, my husband would come in the morning to walk Nico to school, but this is a habit we quickly abandoned. These days, before he opens my fridge, my husband asks: 'May I?'

Quickly, we are getting to know each other less. I don't know what he's thinking. What he's doing. I try to gather an update in the ten minutes we cross paths, but he's not willing to tell me much. Bumping into each other in the same old cafe has become rare, and when it happens, I feel like I'm giving him an interview of some kind. I am embarrassed and shy. He barely answers me, and clearly against his will. It's like an interview with someone who I'm not interested in and who isn't kind to me. My husband doesn't ask me anything. He doesn't ask me if I'm writing, what kind of jobs I'm beginning or ending. He doesn't ask what I'm thinking. We swap information about Nico and plan ahead as much as we can. So, as the sun rises, he disappears into a distance that no longer allows me to see him with clarity: he becomes a shadow, a stain. A stain I could love, maybe?

'Can you pick Nico up to take him swimming?'

'Yes.'

'Everything OK?'

'Everything's OK.'

I still have the photographs and the letters, and, of course, I have Nico. And all the other marks that are left when you lose access to the greatest love of your life to date. Or what used to be: I know that our love used to exist, but I no longer have access to it. Sometimes I am distraught at the thought of this, other times it feels like a new, simple physiological development. Like putting things to bed. Like winter.

'Stop texting me at night, please,' my husband tells me one evening.

'What do you mean?' I ask.

'We're no longer together; you should consider that it might be unsettling to me or my girlfriend to have you intrude on our intimacy.'

'All right,' I say.

I go over the things we've been saying in therapy all too recently. We will always be united, we are not like the others. I try to accustom myself to his request for no more evening messages, adapting once more to the idea that we are different. Only, this time, it also means that we two, *between us*, are not the same, as well as being unlike everyone else. I compare these thoughts to my plants now, in winter, as they remain motionless in a sort of freezeframe, needing care nonetheless. I still wonder what my husband ate this evening, sometimes. I wonder if his new lover is a good kisser. I am genuinely curious. If I'm not able to understand him, if I lose track of what we have done and what is currently happening, all will be wasted. How can I look after my plants if I don't know their names? If I push my husband away completely, then we'll have lost everything. Perhaps, in this distance, I can find the right place to grow my own roots, and know I will continue to exist even if he no longer knows who I am.

'Is it a good time to speak?' I ask him, now and then.

'Not now,' he always says.

Messages are no longer allowed at all. Emails are not allowed either. Looking into each other's eyes is no longer possible. We cannot speak and this is our new geography.

Can I pop round to see how the plants are doing? Maria texts. Maria always asks before she comes to visit. I never think about it, never ask her to come. Her visits are a private matter between her and the plants and I'm only the throughline. They're not my plants, they are hers. Though

Maria would say they don't belong to her either, but to themselves. I host them in winter, spring and summer. Even when she is abroad or travelling, Maria writes to ask how the plants are doing.

Hi Anna,

I wanted to mention that you should check the plants that don't receive water directly when it rains – the ones on the small lower balcony that are sheltered by the metal canopy. I'm thinking specifically about three of the pots: the window box and the two round ones. Water them a little if they look very dry; do it in the morning, on a day when the temperatures don't look to be freezing. Has the hellebore flowered yet? I'm keeping an eye on the weather over there. Kisses, Maria

Maria has saved our city as a location on the weather app on her phone; she always checks it when she is away.

I don't think it'll rain tomorrow, she texts me as soon as she is back in the city.

We'll be waiting for you, I reply.

So Maria comes, and when she arrives, she is excited to see how the plants are doing. She wants to see if the corpses are still corpses, because you never know; to check that the water pipes haven't frozen over, and whether the pots are getting enough nutrients. She takes care of another clean-up and some repotting. The plants are sleeping now, so they suffer less when she moves them.

'Transferring a plant to a new pot while it's in bloom', she says, 'is like asking a pregnant woman to move houses.'

Maria explains that outdoor plants grown naturally in full soil have many ways to access the resources they need, because there the earth is full of life. There are fungi, even worms, that can aid the flow of nutritious substances. This doesn't happen when a plant is grown in a pot, which is why it needs to be organically fertilised.

'Sometimes in a potted plant, the roots will take up all the space, eating up all the soil. When this happens, the roots start looping onto themselves, in tighter and tighter circles, until they close up into themselves completely. That's why you need space, earth. New soil too.'

the roots start looping onto themselves

I, on the other hand, when Maria arrives, am excited to see how *she* is doing. If her health is still good, her body strong, whether she's still suffering for the end of her love. How long her hair is. I want to check whether we're all managing not to close up into ourselves completely.

'Sometimes, just when you think a dry plant is dead, it puts out small new leaves. Before they die, plants go into a sort of stand-by, or convalescence,' Maria explains. 'Sometimes for up to a year. The first thing a plant does when it senses danger is to stop its growth. Take your strawberry tree and your feijoa, for instance: they've put out new buds and they'd been in a coma for ages.'

Maria is always bringing me something new. Plants she grows herself or buys at plant fairs and nurseries outside the city. The plants she brings me usually range between two and ten euros. They're teeny tiny and haven't even begun to develop properly yet.

'Everyone's in a hurry, they want to buy the big plants. Call it plant-à-porter. It's OK to buy a bigger plant now and then to speed things up or cover a gap – I get that – but I like to watch a plant sprout new life and grow right in front of my eyes. I like to find out how a plant will grow in my company as opposed to the company of someone else. To find out what things we can do together. When you buy a plant at the peak of its beauty, you should know you'll be forced to witness its decline. It's like choosing to experience old age instead of youth.'

I'd have liked bigger plants at first. To cover the gaps, at least, and for a little instant gratification. I would have liked flowers, immediately, but we're planting seeds instead and then we'll have to wait and see. When you're growing something, you can never be sure that it will grow at all, or grow in the right way. Like you can't guarantee that love will lead to something. That the sun will rise tomorrow, et cetera.

'I've planted you a winged spindle that will turn bright pink in the winter, and a golden privet – it's a smaller size than the common type. A few perennials too.'

'When do they start growing?'

'In spring, until it gets very hot. Then they'll slow down a bit, and pick up again towards the end of summer. After that they begin to gradually shut down as we get into winter. The aerial part of the perennials disappears in winter, but they're still active under the earth and will pop out again year after year.'

'How big do they get?'

'A little less than they would outdoors, in full soil, and a little less than you're imagining right at this moment.'

Meanwhile, my son and my boyfriend are beginning to get to know each other. Nico doesn't know he's my boyfriend at first, and he welcomes him as a friend among friends. He and I live in two different cities and two different countries, and so we too need to work out a way to be together. A car is not enough, and a train is not enough. It always takes a plane. Meeting up, leaving each other: this keeps happening to us without end. We miss each other. We get used to the absence. We hate it. We think it could work out well. Then we think perhaps it won't work at all. We are getting to know each other while he and my son get to know each other. There are wives and husbands and children with us. In everything we do, every little choice, there are always many people involved – even when he and I are alone, they're still all very much there. When my boyfriend and I are alone together, the absence of our children is a very prominent thought. Seeing him and Nico together warms my heart and makes me wish for things that I feel I should fight against. Living with him somewhere else. Living with him at my flat. Living with him at his house. Us two, living together in our very own home. The very word: home.

My boyfriend has bought some sunflower seeds and he and Nico plant them on the terrace together. The packet says 'giant sunflowers'. It seems like a big claim to make, even in the context of a forest made up of both plants and feelings. My boyfriend and my son are running around among the pots and along the communal walkways, scattering seeds everywhere. My boyfriend doesn't love Nico as if he were his own boy. I don't love his sons as if they were mine. We don't take each other's kids swimming. Or to the doctor's. Or to visit friends. We have no shared habits and we're always missing somebody. We're always having to ask for permission if we're taking a trip or wanting to sleep in a different place. We can't decide by ourselves. *It takes no time to destroy, it is very long to create.*

'Where did you plant them?' I ask.

'It's a secret,' Nico says.

'It's a secret,' my boyfriend confirms.

I like the idea of a secret that's been planted only to be found out. Sooner or later, the truth will come out and it will be a flower. A big yellow one.

Watching a Tree Grow

The days are getting longer, and a few leaves are beginning to sprout in the pots.

'Can you pick up Nico on Wednesday evening? I'm going to London,' I ask my husband, each time I leave.

'Of course,' he always says.

Before I leave, I feel scared. Nico seems the most vulnerable he's ever been. His tonsils are swollen, or he speaks like he has a sore throat. I convince myself he isn't sleeping well and check on him multiple times during the night. The morning of my departure I set the table with extra care. I check the spoon: I want it to be perfectly parallel to the plate. I think that we'll never see each other again. I wonder if he'd remember me, as an adult, were I to die tomorrow. I count the number of biscuits he eats and check how much milk he is drinking. Is he eating less than usual? Is he eating more than usual? Will he be sick while I am away? If he died, how would I kill myself?

'Are you good?' I ask him a hundred times.

'I'm good,' Nico answers me.

'Good like perfect?'

'Good like perfect,' he confirms.

'I'll be back in three days,' I explain. And we count the days on our fingers.

'That's not many,' Nico always says, and he always says that even when we count seven or eight.

'Shall we talk on the phone?' I suggest.

'Let's hug,' he says, and he hugs me very tightly. I kiss him and nibble him and letting him go is unnatural.

Nico never calls me while I'm away. If his father suggests it, 'Shall we call Mummy?', he says no. When he's with me and I suggest, 'Shall we call Daddy?', he also says no. If I'm the one calling, all he says is, 'I love you Mummy, bye bye.' He's not sad: they tell me he doesn't ask after me, that he is happy and kind. Once the plane takes off, I'm not sad either. I'm good. I work. I can focus. I almost write. Sometimes, in fact, coming home is a chore. Yet when I land, with the happiness of hugging Nico again comes a new curiosity to check on the plants. I also think about the plants while I'm away, insisting to people they go by to water them and check how they are. As I'm flying above the clouds, I wonder if a new flower has blossomed, and if it's yellow, pink or whichever other colour.

'If you don't kiss me, I dies,' says Nico one evening as he's falling asleep.

'If you don't kiss me, I die,' I correct him, kissing him. I only correct the verb because I agree with the sentiment.

'Without kisses, the body gets sick. Worst of all in the legs,' he specifies.

When they talk about the days they spent in the hospital, Maria and Alessandro always begin with the fact that somebody else had to take care of washing them and moving their bodies. They both say that there was nothing awkward about somebody washing you like you were a baby – even your privates.

'You're not a man or a woman. You're a body, and your penis, your tits are a part of that system of flesh and bones. They have no additional meaning,' Maria says.

Being a baby, being dependent on someone, needn't be a sad thing, they explain. It's care. It feels good when they touch you. If you don't kiss me, I dies. Say my name. Hug me.

'That summer, after I came home from hospital,' Alessandro tells me, 'I couldn't do anything. I couldn't even stand up. I was staying with my parents and once a week the ambulance drove me over to the hospital to change my dressings. Sometimes a friend came to visit. There was air conditioning both at home and in the hospital, but it was hot outside as we crossed those few metres in the courtyard, while they moved me to the ambulance on a stretcher. The air outside was so muggy, so clearly not controlled with a little remote: it was pure life. Everything was suspended: my relationship with Diana, my work, needing to worry about my future in any other way that wasn't breathing and simply being there. My happiness wasn't dependent on any of those things. I feel a great nostalgia about those months.'

Asking Alessandro and Maria to tell me about those months has something to do with nostalgia for me too. But I am now also nostalgic for places I've never been to. Places I won't be in two hundred years. Places I've not been to in these thirty-six, three hundred thousand years. I miss all the children I'm not having. The books I'm not writing and all of the elsewheres I will never experience nor be able to tell stories about.

In simply needing to breath, to be there, Alessandro felt as if he were a child, or a really old man: there was no other sense to life except for living it. This is when I realise my grandmother has become an old woman. It has happened across a whole lifetime, but, for me, it has happened all in one day. My grandmother has been away for a holiday in the mountains, she has slipped and cracked a rib. The pain in her rib and the fall seem to have aged her from a mature lady into an old woman. Since the accident, she's not been looking after her hair. There's a plaster on her toe. Her feet are swollen. Her hearing is worse. Her hands are trembling. She's sadder. For a woman who wishes to be dead every time she catches the flu, a cracked rib represents the abyss.

'When are Nico's babysitter's twins due?' she asks. But Nico's babysitter isn't expecting twins.

'Are you going to Rome tomorrow?' she asks me right after I tell her I'm going to London.

Repeating things becomes mandatory. So does reminding myself that she will not remember them, that her eyesight is going, as well as her hearing and even her sense of smell.

Every experience appears to her as if dimmed by a patina of distance, which is her old age. Cataract vision. From her perspective, Rome and London are interchangeable, the next pair of twins on the planet is irrelevant, details are just details. She plays cards with Nico and they like the same things. Vanilla ice-cream. The engravings on the wooden domino tiles and playing the piano with two fingers.

'Is your kid eating well?' she asks me. All her life she's asked the same question to every mother she has ever met, including her daughter and granddaughters. When we go out to the public gardens, and a mother sits down next to her, my grandmother asks, 'Is your kid eating good?'

'Quite good,' I say, though Nico doesn't eat much at all.

'Is he sleeping good?'

'He sleeps a lot,' I smile to her. 'I have to wake him up in the morning.'

'*Che bel visin.*'

We, too, used to be *cute little faces*; now it's Nico's turn. Sometimes my grandmother says that getting old is a terrible thing, because her friends are constantly complaining about their illnesses and pains. When I look at her thinning hair, I see mine. She says that her friends are fat, and she's proud that she is not. She says, I can still fit into this dress that is thirty-six years old. I can fit in this skirt that is forty-six years old. I can fit into these trousers that are twelve years old. I'm equally impressed by the fact that she fits in all these forty-six-year-old skirts, and the fact that she can remember how old all her clothes are. How can she? Is it better to be precise than blurry, in her own version of the story? Sometimes my grandmother tells me that everything's moving too quickly, and that she still wants to live for a very long time. I, too, want to live for a very long time and I certainly don't want to be fat like her friends.

'I change my bedsheets on Monday,' my grandmother explains. 'Except sometimes I don't, because the week just hasn't lasted long enough. It can't already be Monday again.'

She always tells me about what she has eaten that day, and what she's about to eat later. She's happy when she makes herself buttered noodles in the evening and she is happy that, for thirty years, she has only ever eaten yogurt with walnuts, honey and raisins for lunch.

'Nice legs,' she says when she looks at me.

'Sort your hair out,' she says.

'Do you have a new ring?' she asks, taking my hands. She turns them over, studies them.

I look at her fingers that have become crooked, and I look at her rings too. I ask her to tell me who gave them to her and when. We talk about my old plants and her new plants, which she keeps on the smaller balcony of her new home.

'I've only got room for a few little pots now,' she says.

My grandmother has always kept seasonal flowers in blossom, in each of her houses. Huge plants. Metres-wide maples. When I'd just had Nico she came to sort through the small pots in my kitchen, swapping the dead plants for new baby ones. That was her gift to me for Nico's birth. Now it's time for small pots for her, filled with annual blossoms. She no longer has the time to watch a tree grow.

'Your mother was unlucky in love,' my grandmother always tells me. 'But at least her love was a great love. Like mine. You, on the other hand, are happy, even though you and your husband have decided to split up.' When she tells me this, it makes me sad. I'd like to be able to reply that mine was a great love too.

Sometimes when it's just Nico, my grandmother, my mother and me, I feel like I'm looking at different degrees of attachment to life, at least partly determined by the levels of perception in our bodies. Our ability to perceive taste; how many of our tastebuds we have already exhausted. For Nico, everything is full of colour, sound and promise. Everything has a special taste and his heart beats fast, like that of a puppy dog. I come next, then my mother, and so on and so forth. Thirty years of age, sixty, eighty. We perceive the colour red less and less. It becomes a pasty pink. Real cataract vision, crooked fingers with a weak grip that tremble while we play cards or dominoes – all of us playing a different game. All of us trembling in our own way. Nico, because he can't quite coordinate his movements yet, my grandmother, because she is old, me, because of my anxiety.

'Stick the cat next to the cat,' we say to Nico.

'This game has such beautiful drawings,' my grand-mother says.

'Don't ruin the tiles,' my mother begs. 'We've had this game since you were kids.'

'Nico, focus,' I tell him. 'That's a panda, not a cat.'

And since Nico is asking, the three of us tell him what a panda is, and what it eats.

'What's bamboo?' he asks. So the three of us explain what bamboo is. Meanwhile, I take out my contact lenses, and try to get used to a blurry life.

A Perfume That Is Potential, Far Away, to Be Sought

My mother is in India, following the Roland Ultra. Sometimes she sends me a picture of a cow, or a self-portrait in which she is wearing a builder's hat made of scrap newspaper, with a caption saying it's very hot. The containers arrive later than expected, so the trip is delayed. In the photographs, my mother looks happy, her teeth exposed in a smile, her eyes narrowed by the sun. Sandy, yellow roads stretch out busily behind her. Meanwhile, over here, the days are getting milder, and so we go back to eating out on the terrace. If I am eating alone, I listen to the laughter of the children from the schoolyard next to the flat. They take their morning break at the same time I get hungry. I always try to pick out Nico's voice among the others, but I never succeed.

'Has Mum called?' we siblings ask one another.

'She sent me a pic of her wearing a paper hat.'

'She sent it to me too, and pictures of cows.'

Our family often falls out of touch – we can spend

months far away from each other. My father, especially: often we don't hear from him at all. It doesn't sound great when I tell people about it, and perhaps it's not been so great to experience it either, but we are used to it. He got us used to it.

'Your father called me to help with his terrace,' Maria tells me.

'Will you take care of it?' I ask.

The fact that she might help him makes me feel both happy and possessive. Maria will be busier. My father's terrace is my father's terrace. I've only visited his house twice in my entire life. Perhaps there is an irrigation system that connects us all, and Maria is putting it to work, but my own tap feels so far away from his end that it's impossible to make sense of the ramifications of the pipes in between.

'Yes, I will take care of it,' Maria replies.

'What are his plants like?' It is possible that my tone sounds the same as the one you'd use to ask after an ex-partner's new girlfriend. What's she like? Tall? Skinny? Pretty?

'Mostly fruit trees. It's a real man's balcony,' Maria laughs.

'How many?'

'Lots for a ten-square-metre terrace. There's a pomegranate, a fig, an apple tree, a persimmon, an apricot tree, wild strawberries and regular strawberries, white grapes and black grapes, an almond tree, a peach tree and a quince, a feijoa, even raspberries. The gardener who used to look after the plants has tied the trees back against the wind, but the ties are strangling them.'

'Which trees are the sickest?' I ask. I'm not even sure why I care about which of his trees are sick, but I do.

'There's brown rot on the apricot, and the pomegranate is struggling to breathe the most.'

'Wasn't he moving out?' I ask.

'There are boxes of books everywhere, but he's not moving yet.'

Maria already knows more about my father than I do. Is it a man's thing to have many fruit trees? To tie them so tight they can't breathe? I've been receiving fruit trees as a gift lately: my new boyfriend buys them for me. A lemon tree, a fig. They're still small. I put them out on the terrace, and we connect them to the irrigation system. I ask Maria to show me how to add a pipe, to combine joints and drippers – how the whole system works. I watch her work several times, without understanding. I'm not a natural, but I can learn. It is important to remember simple things that wouldn't naturally come to mind, such as the fact that water travels down and not up. So it's important to avoid forcing the water to go up and then down in the pipes. It is also important to know that an irrigation system should be checked in reverse order: if water is running out of the last segment, it means all the parts before are free and working well. Once it's been installed, an irrigation system must be frequently checked, especially in the beginning, when you should keep a close eye on it for a few days. The wind changes, and so does the weather: that's why you must keep watch. Another rule is watering less but more frequently. Very few plants like to sit in standing water.

They like water, but they don't like swimming in it.

'Remember to change the battery before you leave this summer,' Maria tells me. On my terrace, she discovers little wild strawberries hidden behind the rosemary bush.

'How would you like some vegetables out here?' she asks me. 'Aubergines make really nice flowers.'

Nico likes to grow things he can look at and smell. He'd sure like to grow something he can eat. Maybe it will encourage him to try new flavours, since there is so little he likes to eat. So, Maria plants some tomatoes and aubergines. Everything's tiny. Nothing exists yet. The new plants have a perfume that is still only potential, far away, to be sought.

'Sometimes I organise gardening workshops for schools,' Maria explains, while we eat.

I've made tomato spaghetti and perfumed it with basil from the terrace. She has dressed the table with a new jar full of twigs and leaf cuttings. We're sitting in front of each other with the windows open.

Maria's hair has grown even longer, and she has lost weight. She is wearing a thin shirt over her wide breasts. She likes eating. I pour her a glass of water. We are two very different women. She isn't vain. She'd talk to anyone. She's kinder than me.

'There are some kids, though, that I just can't stand. I can't even pretend to. The other day I was meant to look after this class of kids and I didn't allow one of the boys to be class leader purely because I found him annoying,' she says.

We dish out seconds. We drink water. Together, we are very hungry and very thirsty. I'd like an ice-cold beer. I'd like some red wine. Some chocolate. I'm feeling good. We're good.

'I'd quite like to host a kids' gardening workshop on my terrace,' I say, on the spur of the moment. 'All about vegetables.'

Sure, I'd also like to repaint the doors of Nico's school, improve their courtyard and sign Nico up for a Chinese-language course. I'd like to open an original-language-only cinema venue. Volunteer. Call the council about that sidewalk covered in dog poop that must have slipped off the mayor of Milan's map of duties. I'd like to be good at many things of this kind that can help and change a school, a neighbourhood, a city, even my family. What about the universe? History?

I feel, though, that the vegetable workshop idea might really please Nico, who is always hoping for other kids to visit him at home. I know he wishes he had a brother: he doesn't want to be alone. If I believe I'd be willing to look after three billion kids on Earth – his brothers, my children – perhaps I could begin by hosting six or seven of them on my terrace, for one hour a week.

Sometimes in the morning Nico wakes me up with his eyes full of tears.

'I want a brother,' he says. I hadn't considered that, when my husband and I split up: I didn't think it would mean that Nico couldn't have a brother or sister. 'I don't want to be alone,' he explains.

'Where would we put him?' I laugh, knowing he's right.

He's right to feel lonely. He is alone. We're all connected by this watering system, and OK, it's a great system, but Nico's pot is his own pot. His terrace his terrace. It has boundaries, a specific quantity of soil and limited room for growth. Do we all belong to an infinite garden, of which each of us tends only to a fraction?

'I could make room for him in in my bed,' Nico suggests, brightening up.

He tried to convince me in the same way he tries to convince me to buy him more Lego, but this time he puts much more intensity in each of his words and his eyes.

'Please,' he says. 'Please, Mummy.'

'I don't know how to do it, Nico,' I explain. 'Dad and I are no longer together.'

'Then you do it,' he says, and keeps crying. 'Please.'

I grew up in a family with many brothers and sisters, and my mother and my father living under the same roof. When I watch Nico seeking love from my new boyfriend, or he tells me he wishes Dad still lived with us, I understand what he means. How can one stand not having a brother when they could have had one? How can one choose not to have a baby if Nico's loneliness is at stake, now and forever? My mother tells me about her own loneliness as an only child, as a young girl and later on, when she had to look after my grandfather alone, then his factory and his legacy.

'When I was a young girl and they went out, I waited for them by the lift, motionless, for two or three hours. I'd fall asleep there.'

'Are you crying?'

'Don't be silly.' She's crying.

My husband and I often tell each other we should have had at least two children. Especially given how things turned out between us. I imagine most people would think the opposite, given how things turned out between us. But it makes sense to us: two children would stick together through their parents' break-up; they wouldn't be alone their whole life. We'd have two children in the house, not one. Guilt would exist in a less absolute sense. Everything would be easier, and we wouldn't have to experience this continuous state of melancholy. But what about our routine? Money. Dressing and undressing two kids in the pool before and after swimming. But in so far as feelings and emotions go, much, much better.

Having other children with our new partners seems harder. Particularly now, when everything's up in the air: the set-up, the routine – planes, houses, plant pots – and it's a hard thing to explain to Nico. It's a hard thing to explain – to ourselves, even – and anyway, it wouldn't be the kind of brother Nico is imagining. A brother and a sister with the same mother and father, the same set of grandparents, who live in the same houses, sharing toys between them across the same set of rooms. Nico will never have a brother like that.

'Well, do you wanna do it now?' my husband and I said, after we broke up.

'Why not?' we answered in turns.

After a while, though, it stopped being funny. The sentence acquires the noise of nails on a blackboard. My stomach seizes up. He stops hugging me. He no longer uses the short version of my name. He says it in full and with a different voice: I have a new identity. In the beginning, I still call him my love. He no longer calls me love. I stop too. Love. Home. Us. I'm coming. Lost words.

'I'm not sure I necessarily want children,' Maria says as we finish the spaghetti. We've become closer. We talk about plant projects and about how our lives are changing. What it is that we're find interesting at the moment, where we have eaten or travelled to lately. I watch her body change, as it reacquires its strength and health, and her mind makes room for calm in place of fear. We talk about films we should see in the cinema, and new bars that have just opened. We broaden our horizons – our garden. Maria wants to go to America; she has applied for a bursary to provide horticultural therapy at some hospitals there. We look up the pictures of the hospital management, the woman director with wild hair; we study the climate in Portland and find a fun TV series on the internet called *Portlandia*, in which everyone is so kind nobody ever crosses the road because they won't do it before others have crossed first. Maria and I like each other, we're good together, but we only see each other when she comes to look after the plants. We wouldn't think of going out for a beer together. We need our forest.

'I find it baffling that people expect you to necessarily want children,' Maria continues. 'A friend of mine just had a baby and the first thing she said to me after the birth – she was serious, too, all pumped with adrenaline – was,

"You'll see, Maria, soon you'll find a great guy so you can also have a baby." I just couldn't believe it. What a thing to tell someone!'

She looks at me expectantly. I don't have an opinion. Though I can imagine what kind of adrenaline her friend was on, and what tone she might have used to try and elicit Maria's jealousy. Is Maria insisting that she doesn't necessarily want to have children because of her own doubt, or because of her own certainty? Do I want a baby with another person? If I'm in love with someone, must I have children, or desire a different home?

I've always been told that my grandmother was unhappy about each of my mother's pregnancies. She got mad every time my mother announced a new baby. When I tell my mother that Nico really wants a brother, she either asks, 'Are you writing?' or suggests, 'Let's buy him a puppy.' She doesn't like the idea of me making a brother for Nico.

'Would he live in Milan or in London?' my boyfriend and I sometimes ask each other, laughing.

We don't really believe we will have a baby, but we are very much in love by this point, so sometimes we think about names, as people who are very much in love often do. He tells me: I want your baby. I want a piece of you. Will you make me a baby? Can I? Will you make me a little girl? I'd love to have a little girl all our own. Let's call her Maria. Or Lola. My new boyfriend has two children, he lives in a different city; I have one child, I live in this city. It's all upside down, in actual fact. Would a child of our own change the love between us, as happened for both of us with our previous partners, when we had our firstborns? Would I stop loving him too?

'Be careful,' I tell him, then. Even though sometimes I wish he weren't careful. On the other hand, if I hadn't said 'Be careful,' then he probably wouldn't ask, 'Can I?'

In the evening, Nico wants to read books about making children. Sometimes these books say that children are made when the joy between two people reaches a peak. That's what the books say: their joy reached a peak. Does that mean that the sexual education books are claiming that one is less happy after having a baby? That making a baby is peak joy and, afterwards, you can only really come down from that high? Nico and I study the pictures of dividing cells: two, four, hands, feet. The mum goes to hospital to give birth and the dad is standing next to them as it happens.

'Does the little seed break?' Nico asks, looking at the pictures.

'It doesn't break. It divides itself to make the baby,' I say.

'Can you make a thousand babies in one go in the egg?'

'No. But one by one you could still make a lot of them.'

'How many?'

'Even twenty.'

'I will make twenty.'

When I tell Maria about 'peak joy' according to Nico's books she reminds me about plant-à-porter.

'What was plant-à-porter? I can't remember,' I say.

'It's like peak joy in plants!' she smiles. 'Remember? Buying them at the peak of their lives, and so agreeing to witness their inevitable decline. It doesn't make much sense as a project, does it?'

Nico comes back from school and Maria shows him what's new on the terrace. This, too, becomes a habit, and the two of them develop a relationship with the plants, independent from mine. Nico shows Maria the secret spots in which the sunflowers are growing. She'd already noticed them, but she pretends to see them for the first time. Each sunflower is growing at a completely different pace from the others. In some of the pots, they have barely sprouted; in others, they've put out robust, wide leaves. Like Nico, in nursery school, looking for a place to settle down so he wouldn't feel restless.

At the end of her working day, Maria walks around the terrace and along the balconies, her gaze lost in the plants. She is talking about them, telling me what's going on. Sometimes she pauses to pick up a twig, study a leaf or tell me what her dreams for our future are, and explain what is about to happen. She comes down with the buckets, the shears, all her tools, and loads them into her red Fiorino. Nico and I like to watch her get in the van and circle the square in the direction of her home. After the split with her boyfriend, Maria has gone back to living outside the city. Her new house was practically in ruins; now she has very many plants.

'Not as many as you're imagining,' Maria tells me. 'Many, many more.'

So I start imagining her house as a forest, like the ones in the fairy tales, full of butterflies, birds, bunnies and all sorts of wild things. I imagine that the animals speak to Maria, as if she were Snow White, helping her with her house chores, in her ruined house turned castle. Maria is a cartoon character. Everything is alive and bright, and blackbirds are sitting on her shoulders as Nico and I often wish they would do with us; they even help tidy the house and make the beds.

'Last winter, a mouse ate the front paws of my tortoise,' she tells me one day, interrupting my Snow White reverie. 'I have to give her injections now. She'll always have stumps. I need to find a cat to kill the mice. I wouldn't ever *buy* a cat though, so it's more complicated than you'd think.'

the stumpy tortoise

As Maria puts her coat back on, she bids me and the plants goodbye several more times. I don't think she really wants to leave: if she stayed here for a few days in a row, she could do so many more things, and she knows it. We almost never have all the time that is needed to build, to borrow the words of Mr Bharat. It's not easy to say goodbye to the plants and see them again only after time has passed. Saying goodbye to Nico and not seeing him each time I go away on a trip.

'Plants arranged in a specific order, or too symmetrically, really freak me out,' says Maria, whenever we're looking at the balconies on the other side of my flat where my neighbour keeps the ivy trimmed back into a perfect square frame, surrounding a row of alternating flowers and ball-like boxwood shrubs.

'She's probably so proud of them,' I say.

'On the other hand, we probably freak *her* out.'

Sometimes Maria and I enjoy discussing our thoughts on order and disorder, on balcony-specific points of view, on what frightens us when it comes near or far, and all one can learn from looking at people's balconies, terraces, gardens and pots, and how their respective owners take care of them. We're feeling better and better.

'You'll have a little girl,' the psychic whispers in London.

'I don't want to,' I say, almost immediately. I open my eyes and stand up.

'It'll be very easy, actually. And anyway, you don't have a choice.'

'I wouldn't know where to put her. Maybe at Heathrow airport.'

'Great idea, you'll enjoy living there,' she laughs. 'The only problem is all those perfumes they sell. Do you mind strong smells? I always get a headache when I walk through duty-free.'

As she says this she lights up ten, twenty, thirty incense sticks and I start to cough. The perfumes of the duty-free in Heathrow mingle with the incense smoke, filling up my nostrils.

'I have a headache,' I say.

'You're just a little scaredy-cat,' she maintains. 'It's really easy to make you believe things.' I try not to have a headache. Not to cough. Not to be someone who easily believes things. 'Sit down,' the psychic says.

I sit down, and a silver airship appears again before my eyes, but I make it disappear by coughing harder. I see my boyfriend. Quickly, he disappears too.

'I'd like to go out dancing with you,' the psychic adds. 'But I'd also like you to learn to park.'

'OK,' I say. She hugs me again while I'm choking.

'It's me, your little girl,' she says. 'You've been waiting for me.'

'Really?' I wheeze. I'm running out of breath.

'Don't you see you scare easy?' the psychic says. 'Don't you see how easy it is to make you believe things?' and she starts laughing.

In All Corners, Strong, Everywhere

At night, Nico tells me: 'I am happy because I love you and I love you because I love you.' Now the sunflowers are growing faster than the eye can see. The secret invented by my boyfriend and Nico – that secret devised just to be found out – is exploding into bloom. Each morning, Nico and I wake up and immediately check on the sunflowers. One of them appears to be aiming for the sky: its stem is so thick that it's beginning to look like a tree trunk.

'If it gets big enough, we could put a chair on top of it,' Nico suggests.

There are caterpillars living in the branches and leaves, and butterflies often visit our terrace. Birds sweep down to say hi. Maria sends me an email. Actually, she sends it to Nico.

Hi Nico,
The butterfly that visits your terrace that we saw the other day is called a 'peacock butterfly' (*Aglais io*). If you want, you can register your terrace as a butterfly 'oasis'

on this website. Butterfly oases are green corridors in the city that help butterflies survive, jumping from terrace to garden and from a balcony to another. If you do it, I'll help you identify the plants I think they like. Kisses, Maria

I'm thinking I'd like to have a green corridor of my own like the one the butterflies use to cross the city, to move between one family and the other; from a family of mine to another family of mine. A functional channel in which I am always safe from harm. Nico and I imagine planting trees to add shade to our terrace, but the flooring is so thin that it would probably collapse on his head. Nico's bedroom sits below the terrace, and he likes that: he likes that the sky is right above him, instead of another flat. He says there are plants growing on top of his head.

As soon as the stones get warmer, the lizards arrive. Wild weeds are growing in the gaps of the tiles; we should keep them in check, but it's just too much fun discovering them. Moss, mint and butter bush are everywhere. The wall of the house is becoming covered with climbing vines and looks less old. The echinacea, the catnip and the other gramineous grasses are bulking up: they are well fed and ready to blow up. Well-fed plants – that's what Maria calls them and now I call them that too. The blackbird comes to visit often. We greet it each morning, slowly opening the door to the terrace and taking a few steps towards it until it flies away. After a few days, we learn to approach it without making it flee.

'It feels like a holiday being out here,' our guests tell us when they come to visit.

Nico asks me if he can hang around on the terrace naked. He can. So he gets naked. If we're alone I get naked too. We put two small white recliners between the winged spindle and the oleander. We buy a wooden table that sits eight and an outdoor lantern to light up in the evening. Six green metal chairs. Maria taught me to say 'winged spindle'.

When it was still cold, my husband wrote HELP with a piece of chalk on one of the terrace tiles. It doesn't come off. It stays on the tile throughout the seasons, come rain or shine. HELP. Every time I read that word, it makes me afraid, and, each time, it takes on a new meaning. Maybe the word will disappear when I've found a solution, and my husband will no longer need help. When Nico asks me why Dad wrote HELP on the tile, I always tell him a different thing. A chair had fallen on his foot. It was raining and he was locked out up here. Martians were coming and they wanted to kiss him on the mouth, with their green Martian tongues.

There are more flowers now, more sunny hours and more hours of peace in our hearts. The lemon tree puts out a lemon. The fig tree two figs. Nico is like the mint: in all corners, strong, everywhere. He's in every pot, spreading quicker and smelling better than all of the other plants.

'When I go to the market or to the plant nursery, I never know what to buy,' I tell Maria on the phone.

'Think about a plant's eventual full size, but as for the rest you should just buy what you like,' Maria rebuts me, as if it were obvious. 'For instance, you might want to avoid buying a giant redwood tree,' she laughs.

'I can't tell if it's the right season, or if the plants are doing OK. For instance, I saw this thin olive tree that cost twenty euros, and I very nearly bought it, but then I thought you wouldn't approve of it.'

'You're right, actually – it doesn't make sense to grow an olive tree here. It won't grow how you want it. It's about disappointing expectations. You're thinking, I don't know, of olive trees in Puglia, full of singing cicadas. But an olive tree will struggle in Milan and certainly no cicadas will ever live in it.'

'So what makes sense?'

'Generally, not always expecting cicadas to visit.'

As it gets hotter, it rains again, and we experience several thunderstorms. The iris we've planted starts sprouting leaves; I send a photograph of it to Maria. After a few hours, she writes back.

Fancy that iris! Wow! And I can see a nice background of chives too. Can you believe this monsoonic rain? I'll try to swing by this week; it can't rain forever, can it? Kisses, M.

I struggle to picture a time with no more torrential rain. Even though now Maria is stronger. Even though Maria's vein is no longer about to flood her brain, and her pain for the end of her love is dissipating, the downpour is still very much here.

I'm working a lot, and I'm working quickly, fitting in whatever I can: Nico, his hair that needs drying at the swimming pool, storybooks in the evening and then meetings, travelling, writing commissions, and of course my new love, which needs cultivating. Breathing. Trying to sleep at night as opposed to continuing to move boxes in my mind, including the Roland Ultra containers, in India. I try to erase the boxes, objects and names from my mind. Our faces. Even in India, I erase the containers, focusing only on movement itself. On distance as the right distance itself. On the places in which plants grow and blackbirds land. Or the places where printing machines get back to working again, changing name and family, country and time zone. I'm looking for a nameless place, a place without streets, in which none of the boxes has writing on it, or an owner, and each of the game pieces occupies its own role and its own role only: father, son, mother, daughter. I open up my story, lay it open to see. My story's roots are older than me: it comes, then it runs away elsewhere, yielding unexpected results, fruit that I will never eat. That's how I reach a wild thought, which turns out to be a plot – and so together with the new roots and the struggle for light, all at once, summer also arrives. Colours are having it out with the world; so are smells. Windows stay open despite the rain. Words come. So do bees. We take all our clothes off.

'You're beautiful,' Nico says.

'You're beautiful,' I say. Here, hidden away in our forest, nobody can convince us that telling someone they are beautiful is a bad thing.

My mother reaches the end of the Roland Ultra trip. When she comes back from India, she's no longer so stern with me. She gifts us textiles for the flat, even though you can tell she'd rather keep them herself. We try hanging the fabrics on a couple of windows, by a door.

'They're not looking great,' she says.

'I could use them as a bedspread,' I suggest.

'Better not,' she says, wrapping the fabric up again. She's started putting 'I love you' at the end of her text messages again.

Strong winds help me go faster, on my moped or on a plane. When speed turns into turbulence and tremor, I look for a butterfly channel to slip into and avoid catastrophe. I'm flying so much that the flight attendants' faces are becoming familiar. Summer storms are becoming stronger, more frequent.

'What will the weather be like during the flight?' I ask every time.

'All will be well.'

The flight attendants say that even when it's hailing so much that the trees are bent sideways. Even when the plane windows are battered by rain. I want to tell them that it might be better not to answer that all will be well, when we really have no way of knowing; I want to say that all of a sudden, a vein can explode or a lightning bolt strike. Yet each time I nod and smile. And each time I trust them. If the flight attendants say that all will be well, superstitiously, I accept it as fact: one thousand per cent, all will be well. And they are right, all is well, even when there is turbulence and even when I'm scared. Life, after all, seems to function OK, even as you encounter an air pocket, even if there is climate change, even in the twists and turns of the universe. I land. I show my passport at checks. A little booklet that reminds the officers and myself of who I am today. I step onto the airport transfer train that takes me back to a different city, while all of us – Nico and I, me and my husband, my husband and Nico, me and my boyfriend, my boyfriend and his children, and the tens and hundreds and thousands of people who live and breathe on this planet – are hanging in the balance. Europe, the world, the whole universe: we're all on a tightrope and the tightrope is shaky. We have so many feet and so many paws, but, somehow, we have managed not to lose sight of each other. The Roland Ultra has come back to life. My friends are beginning to get to know my new boyfriend. Nico and my boyfriend are getting closer. The sunflowers keep growing taller. Maria has long hair now, like liana: a rope that extends from mountain to mountain. The blackbird gets used to us, and it lets us come closer. Meanwhile, I get closer to everyone else; I hug, I kiss, I say welcome back. I say, I'm back. I say, time to leave again. Whenever I've climbed to a new mountain summit, I take in the new landscape. I call everything and everyone by name.

'I'd like to introduce my new girlfriend to Nico,' my husband says, one day, in the car. We're going to pick up Nico from a party.

'Are you sure?' I say.

I look out of the car window and think about the time I looked out of this very car window on my way to giving birth. We used to call it a space car, perhaps because we'd hoped it could take us all the way to the moon.

'You introduced your boyfriend to Nico,' he points out.

'I'm not worried about appearances,' I blurt out. 'Each new person we love cannot hurt us. Not on purpose anyway. But I'm worried about disappearances.' Though I've just come up with it on the spot, this isn't so bad as a general line of thinking. I decide I'll maintain it from now until the moment I die.

'What are you asking me? I don't understand,' he says.

'Whether she's here to stay.'

He laughs. I laugh too. How are we supposed to know that? How would we know which sunflower will grow the tallest? I can't even remember the names of my plants yet; I don't remember what lies I have been telling up until this point, and which ones I'm still liable to get found out for. Sometimes, in my dreams, I have killed, and so I convince myself that I'll go to jail. If it were up to me, the Roland Ultra would have never gone back to printing: I don't give a fuck about nice Indian gentlemen. I don't even want to make a baby girl for Nico and my boyfriend. Why should I be entitled to give others advice?

'All will be well,' says my husband, in a flight attendant's voice.

None of us is here to stay – isn't that what you're thinking of when you speak this way? I am happy that my husband has found a new girlfriend, because now he is happier. The possibility of his unhappiness scared me more:

I was concerned it would turn into anger, or, worse still, into a fault of mine.

'OK.' I cut things short, and there is silence between us again.

In the evening, I text my husband that I trust him. He replies saying, I trust you too, and we never talk about it again. I never ask Nico about his new girlfriend, just take in the information he mentions among other things: I ate chicken, Giulio was there, Serena was there. Serena gave me a new bow and arrows. Serena taught me how to make tea. Serena has a flat belly. Serena has a sausage dog.

I ask Nico to make me tea in the way Serena taught him. I take a picture of him and send it to my husband.

'Aren't you jealous?' everyone's asking. Anyone, really. Even the bar staff at the cafe we all go to, separately.

'Not at all,' I say, neatly cleaning my coffee cup with the tip of my tongue.

'Dad and Serena had friends over for dinner,' Nico says, more and more often.

'Have you eaten, *bel visin*?'

'I've eaten,' he says.

I'm not jealous. Even when I picture the dinner, and Serena, and our friends together.

'I took the dog out to the park with Serena,' Nico says.

'Is it a nice dog?' I ask.

I'm not even jealous of Serena's dog, though Nico and I wish we had one too. Sometimes people like to tell me that my husband's new relationship is not really a serious one. They tell me: she's pretty, yeah, but you're prettier. They tell me, apparently she's a dancer. Or she's trying to be one. They're hoping to cheer me up, I think, by letting me know I am better or criticising my husband. It doesn't change things for me. Often now I am able to think that Serena is pretty without an immediate need to qualify this thought with feeling or further implications. I insert her in a dance routine I've devised for her in my head, and whenever I mention her, I feel like Antoine Doinel in the Truffaut film, saying 'Antoine Doinel' in the mirror. Serena's name is like background noise, a thought like a repeated sentence, with a sound but not a meaning. Sometimes I worry about her, who's embarked on such a complicated relationship. I hope that my husband will treat her fairly and I even imagine I could help her make sure things go well between them. I'd like to tell her, don't feel like A if he does B. Watch out because when C happens, it will lead to D. Then I think XYZ, and in ideograms. A few odd things happen. For instance, one evening my husband gets angry because I've liked one of Serena's pictures on Instagram. I tell him, look, what the hell are you talking about? She will die, I will die, so will Nico. We're almost gone already. Like flowers. Plants. We are movement. A forest. Instagram?

'How dare you?' my husband says, very seriously.

'Dare doing what?'

'How dare you follow her?'

'When I see her, we shake hands. She spends time with Nico. When we went to therapy, you used to say that you wanted a united and fluid family. Don't you still dream that we could be friends? I say this because I really do hope for that. Do you?' I get angry because my husband's distance doesn't match mine, and so we're both at the wrong distance. How can we understand each other on matters like movement, irrigation systems and butterfly channels? What the blackbird understands, my husband doesn't.

'You mustn't follow her on Instagram,' he insists.

'Never talk to me about Instagram ever again,' I hiss, hanging up in his face. These are the kinds of thoughts I have about my husband and his new partner. Little things. Mostly I hope she is good with Nico, and for other small matters, such as wishing she'll be teaching him Spanish, since she's half-Spanish, or that she won't smoke in front of him, because I know she smokes, or give him her iPad to play with, though I'm not sure she even has an iPad. Trifles, in any case, that are simply to do with another person spending time with your son. A person who, perhaps, is here to stay. Who discusses Instagram with my husband.

'How's it going with your girlfriend?' I ask my husband sometimes.

'Very well,' he says.

Then, if I'm feeling funny, I add, 'How about Instagram? All OK there?'

The psychic squeezes my hand.

'They will break up,' she says.

'No, please!' I say.

'But you'll disappear beforehand,' the psychic starts crying.

'Do you mean I will die?'

'Yes,' she says. 'And me too.'

My husband and I are having breakfast with Nico at our usual cafe, while I'm reading a newspaper article about how the end of a romantic relationship must be dealt with like a loss among many, such as grief or illness. The psychoanalyst who signed the piece says that mediation is something to avoid. You need to put distance between yourselves.

'You'll get back together,' lots of people say.

I pass my husband the paper and tell him to read the piece.

'I don't want to,' he says.

'Please,' I repeat, smiling.

With my eyes, like a mime, I signal that this is important for me. Maybe I'm not a great mime, even though as a child I was sent to Paris to study under Marcel Marceau. But my husband only has eyes for Nico. So on this day, like many others, I ask him why he's avoiding my eyes.

'He's avoiding your eyes because he loves you,' my mother often says.

'If he'd looked me in the eyes, maybe we'd still love each other. If he'd loved me for real, he would've looked at me.'

'It's impossible to talk to you.'

'That's why I'm writing.'

'You're writing? Are you really?' my mother brightens.

'Yes,' I say.

'You're not airing your business in public, are you?' she asks. 'Because who do you think would be interested in your own private business? It should stay like that: private.'

My husband and his girlfriend buy an avocado tree and they're happy. She talks about the avocado. He talks about the avocado. They take photos of the avocado. They look after it and even give it a name. Nico is also talking about the avocado. The avocado has become the centre of a thousand adventures. One day my husband comes to visit me while Maria is there, and admires the plants, exchanging a few words with her. He asks Maria if she can go round to his house to help. Could she look after the avocado tree with a name? Could she care for the avocado that's the centre of a thousand adventures? My husband and his girlfriend have started stocking up on memories. I can tell. They've names for avocado plants together, like he and I had names for our cars, motorbikes and flats. Our space car, versus their avocado. The spoken expressions we've coined in the past. Concepts we've built and shared – our theories. The notes we used to pin around our house. Our I-love-yous; their I-love-yous.

'All I have is an avocado tree,' my husband tells Maria. They laugh. I laugh with them.

'Why are you making that face? It's a beautiful avocado tree.' They're laughing even harder.

'Is that what you need help with?' Maria asks.

'Well, I have three balconies and a mini terrace. I'd like to expand.'

'More avocado trees?'

'Maybe,' my husband says. 'You wanna come check it out?'

So Maria starts looking after my husband's plants too. She cares for his avocado tree. His and his girlfriend's.

My husband tells me that when Nico sleeps over, in the morning he is given the task of misting the avocado tree.

'When he's with me, Nico's more grown up,' he explains. Nico even makes him breakfast now and knows how to toast bread. And, of course, he can make tea like Serena taught him.

'My avocado tree has bloomed and now it's put out four teeny tiny fruits,' my husband tells me one evening.

'That's mad!' I say, and I feel a little jealous of the avocado tree.

'It's really rare! A practical impossibility,' he says. He's in a good mood, happy. He keeps getting better.

'Can I have one as a gift?' I ask him. He does not give me one, and he's right.

Summer, Hail

As summer approaches, Maria tidies the terrace and brings over new plants. The sun hangs closer to us now, and, some days, it burns. The chilli peppers have sprouted, the basil plant is huge and there are roses in every corner of the terrace. The thyme, lavender and sage bushes are stronger than ever. Flowers materialise each in their own colour and shape: yellow, pink, white, sky blue. The grains have multiplied and the purple leaves of the perilla have taken over at least ten of the pots. Perilla? I know how to say perilla now. We need to set a longer timer on the irrigation system, and to lop the lemon tree so the sun can better penetrate its crown. We need to make a start on moving some of the pots. And relocate the azalea to a more shaded spot. The leaves on the smaller wisteria are yellowing; it's thirsty and needs a new place. We're warming up our bones, setting them out to dry in the heat.

When Maria comes to visit me now, she has less time to

spare but we still find a moment to eat outside. I cut beets, cheese and chives. I add rocket and tear leaves from the basil plant to put in the tomato salad. I slip mint twigs into the water jug.

Maria tells me she's been accepted for the American bursary. She'll be joining a hospital that is part of a network of horticultural therapy providers.

'The gardens are there to help both the staff and the patients,' she says. 'They're open twenty-four seven.'

I shake my head, jotting down 'garden', 'therapy', 'care' on an imaginary hand with an imaginary pen. With my imaginary goodwill, I am always promising I'll read through countless notes.

'I'll be gone for three months,' Maria announces.

'Or maybe forever.'

'I don't think so,' she laughs.

The routine of our lunches, her care for our plants, have been one of the few certainties during the past year. Now that we are getting back on our feet, will losing sight of each other mean we will dry up or rot from the inside? Are we each other's butterfly channel?

'Going to America makes me think of my ex-boyfriend. Mostly because he's always on his bike, and I'm moving to bicycle city. They do everything in the way we like it there, and I'll probably feel like I want to tell him about every plant, garden or flower I see. But I'm also thinking that I need to protect my love for plants, even though they make me think of him. That I continue to care about the same things, plants included, makes the distance between us more difficult, but there's little I can do about that,' she says. 'You know what? For a long time all I did was cook and read novels. If I got up at all in the morning, I considered it a special event. He used to tell me I was different. Once he said, you're no longer Maria – that made me real fucking angry. Maybe I was different, but I was still Maria, one thousand per cent. Here I am.'

Maria. Anna. Cherry laurel. Oleander. Winged spindle tree.

I don't ask Maria if she's afraid of going so far, when, until a few months ago, she panicked simply leaving her house. I don't want to put fear in her head if she hasn't thought about it herself. So we laugh one more time about how orderly, organic and civilised every little thing will be out there. About how people, out there, all go about saying, Fantastic! Gorgeous! I'm feeling like a million dollars!

A couple of days later, while I am en route to London, Maria returns to my terrace. In the evening, she sends me an email.

Dear Anna,
The plants are all very well – there have even been three resuscitations! It's so great when the dead come back to life. The only one that's actually dead, I'm afraid, is the strawberry tree: it's all shrivelled up. As I'd foreseen, I didn't quite manage to do all that was needed. I've made a start on cleaning up, got rid of the dry stuff and the broken bits. Weeded here and there, though there are still a lot of abusive residents that need pulling out of all the cracks and crevices. They've come to the party uninvited, and we'll have to kick them out – not to be mean, but they tend

to become unmanageable. Among them, there's a little crooked mulberry, which I'm letting be for the moment, as part of the forest – we'll figure that one out later. The mint is beautiful, as you say, but it's really getting out of control: I'd like to pare it back and introduce something else to its ranks. I've planted another tomato plant in the cement crate, where we'd put the basil, which I've moved somewhere else. I've left the sunflowers where they were. I've only repotted three of them by the door. About the irrigation system: I ran a check and changed a bunch of spritzers, the ones that were missing their plugs, remember? My main suspect is Nico: have you interrogated him? I haven't set the timer yet, but you can water manually for now: you press the button, and it starts. One of the two power banks is unplugged because it needs a new battery, and I hadn't brought one with me. It started saying things to me in German – philosophy, I imagine, but I don't speak the language. I've planted the second wisteria bush, but we'll have to wait for it to grow before it can reach the other side of the window. If it doesn't bloom, it means it's been thirsty in the earlier part of the year. Things I'd like to do next: final touches to the irrigation system, general fertilisation of the soil, reducing the butter bush, repotting the annuals. One final thing: I've pruned back the laurel branches that were full of aphids, and moved it to a sunnier spot so it grows back healthier. I know you don't want gaps, because of Nico, so I've put the toy trolley in front of it to cover the hole for the time being. It's raining here now, you know?
Kisses, M.

I want to put the final touches to the irrigation system and do a general fertilisation of the soil of my life too! My mother calls me. When I tell her about all the metaphors I keep coming up with, she snorts. I keep going until she eventually laughs.

'Have you spoken to your father?' she asks me.

'No, why?'

'Because he's your father?'

I keep feeling an urge to say things about the meaning of life, and the passage of time. I always want to talk about watering and thirst. I keep on telling people about how sunflowers grow differently even when they are planted in identical pots, right next to each other. In order to stop talking about these things, I begin writing with more dedication. I get used to being on the brink of tears all the time, and come up with a theory for this too.

During a couple of work meetings with new people, I burst into tears. It's a sudden emotion that can be triggered by a simple text, a photograph or a song. A word. I'm beginning to worry I might be experiencing a kind of conversion. I hope I don't start believing in God.

In order to feel less ashamed, I expose myself further.

'I'm not sad,' I say, in tears.

I am smiling with my mouth to seem more convincing. Often, I'm crying in front of people I've not met before, and my tears immediately make us intimate. Is this a kind of irrigation too? When the tears reach my lips, I wipe them away with my elbow, looking for a joke to amuse the audience. Maybe they'll talk about me in a year, while I'll be locked up in a sanatorium or a monastery, and say, well, you could tell she wasn't in a good place, she was always crying. And do you remember how she was always talking about sunflowers and thunderstorms?

'You sure won't forget this meeting,' I add, so I can put that thought out of my head too.

During the meetings, I strain to cancel out my tears, archiving them as just another of the day's memories. So, among other things, I agree to write a script about a female songwriter, a TV series on finding happiness in the middle of the financial crisis, a sports TV show, a cultural TV show, and all the while I'm recording voiceovers for talcum powders, cars and reality shows. I get pulled into too many meetings in too many cities I don't really want to go to. I end up talking to people who sell craft beer and people who sell pasta, dishwashers and perfumes. I take too many planes and too many trains. Even the flight attendants are getting fed up with my neediness. Sometimes, without me asking, they tell me: You won't die today, OK?

In the evenings, I tell Nico to come into my bed, pretending it's a treat for his benefit, and I read him the fairy tales that frighten me. If – as often happens in the Brothers Grimm's tales, but even in Roald Dahl's – a story begins with a dead mum, I omit that detail, and I have to come up with a complicated parallel history that I'll have trouble remembering the following day. But how could I suggest to him that death even exists? That death is a certainty? Mine, of all deaths – I could never! There is still a serious possibility that we are both immortal. Or maybe just him.

'Why doesn't his mum help him?' Nico asks when there's no mother in the tale.

'She helps him, but he doesn't realise it,' I try.

'What do you mean she helps him, but he doesn't realise it?'

'To make him grow bigger and wiser the mum takes a step back, so that the little boy has a chance to learn on his own. The more self-sufficient a child is, the smarter he becomes.' I root about in my brain for sentences by Maria Montessori, or Maria the gardener, which I've carried with me since age five and age thirty-five.

'Tell me the truth. Is she dead?'

'Are you actually writing?' I ask myself in my mother's voice, and in mine.

'The mum – she's dead, isn't she?' Nico insists.

'You could put it that way,' I reply. 'But you and I are never going to die, maybe.' And Nico and I fall asleep like that, with all of the voices of the people we love telling us goodnight, sleep tight, don't be afraid of the darkness. Maybe you are never going to die.

'This is not the time to judge your novel!' the psychic says suddenly.

My heart jolts in my chest. The room is filled with incense, so full of smoke I'm not sure there's still a house around it.

'This stuff is too near, too alive. Your priority now is to put down roots. It'll all be fine, but it might take a while.'

The psychic squeezes in closer, shutting her eyes.

'How long?' I ask.

'Do you want a reply like, next Tuesday? Thursday at ten?'

The psychic gives me a head massage as if she were lathering shampoo into my scalp. She's very energetic. I relax, trying to fall asleep again, thinking that, once I exit this room, I will be cleansed, and if I ever look for the psychic again or this particular place, I will never find them again. Better to enjoy it while it lasts.

'Good girl, go to sleep. Na-nite,' she helps me. Then she sings a song by Beyoncé.

My TV series about the couple's break-up is a success. When it's confirmed that it will be renewed for a second season, I'm tasked with writing about their son adjusting to the new situation. I can't stop shaking while I write the words of the little boy who is suffering because of their divorce, who sleeps badly and eats all the time. The little boy in the series doesn't want to sleep at his father's place, and I'm writing that scene at the same time as, for the first time, I am forced to consider the number of days Nico spends with me, and with his father. My husband has developed a whole new interest in dates.

'Nico's doing all right. We're all doing all right for the first time in ages. Are you sure you want to do this?' I ask him.

He insists, and so we talk numbers and dates. We have clearly entered our second act. It isn't very spectacular, as an emotional turning point. Talking dates, bank accounts and Instagram doesn't fit well in the movie of us. The audience would walk out yawning. But since a good denouement works so well that they teach it on screenwriting courses, I commit to it.

'Who are you?' I ask my husband every now and then, and on the one hand I know exactly who he is, and it hurts me. On the other, I am utterly unsure of who he is, and that also hurts me. Sometimes I even ask my boyfriend, 'Who are *you*?' And though I smile at him, I'm not smiling properly because he really is a new face and a new heart by my side, and sometimes his beard, his mouth, his love, all trigger a sort of vertigo in me. Sometimes I really do mean what I say: who are you? I think it violently. I touch my boyfriend with my fingers, I hold him, and cry for the pair of us, so deeply in love with each other, while we remain strangers and will be strangers forever. On Earth, I know Nico and I know my mother. I know my sisters and my brother. My grandmother. No one else belongs to me and I belong to nobody else.

'Who am I?' I ask Nico, then.

'If you ask me that, I get scared,' he says.

I keep writing more episodes of the TV series. Depending on my mood, the two parents are a reasonable couple, or two complete idiots fighting in front of their son.

'Come home to us,' she whispers to him in the fifth episode.

'What are you saying?' her husband says.

'I miss you,' she says. After a short pause, he explains he is no longer in love with her. He's in love with a different girl now. She's a dancer.

Meanwhile, the Roland Ultra is printing cardboard fruit crates. After getting back from the India trip, my mother began working on a great exhibition to be held at her gallery – my grandfather's former factory – with help from the photographer Giovanni Hanninen. They've spread out all the screen-tests on the floor and are dividing them into groups and subgroups. The trip has been turned into a set of various subsets: faces, working men's portraits, children's portraits. Screws. Bolts. Trajectories. Movements. The primary tones in all of the pictures are yellow and brown. Maybe it's the sand, or the cardboard that's fed into the machine, the rust of the bolts, or the colour of people's skin. There are many teeth, Indian smiles, which my mother copies in her photographs taken in India. In the photographs, the Roland Ultra is decorated with paper garlands and flowers, to celebrate its return to life. The female workers are wearing elegant saris as if they were headed to a formal party. The men sit on piles of cardboard, collecting the output of the machine. Nobody would celebrate the Roland Ultra in this way if I hadn't been able to let it go.

All the boys in the pictures, in all pictures from everywhere, are Nico.

Nico and I look at the pictures, and we look at my mother and the photographer as they divide them again and again, parcelling out their trip in new ways. While we watch them work, we understand that infinite associations are possible to create new subsets. My mother and the photographer try them all. By size: big photos versus small photos. Photographs of people and cars. Beautiful and ugly photos. Your family, my family. Connecting the subsets, the dots, is the story. The forest.

'When does a person become an adult?' Nico asks while we look at the pictures. I keep quiet because I've never asked myself this question before, so I don't know the answer. Is it something to do with the wish to have children, to take upon us responsibility for someone else? With independence? Is independence an adult thing?

'I don't know the answer to this one, I'm sorry,' I eventually confess. Nico seems happy all the same. And so am I.

Saving Planet Earth

My brother's daughter is born. They call her Gea. After planet Earth and my grandfather's factory. It's also the name of the therapy centre my husband and I went to, to break up. I rush to meet my brother at the hospital, and I find him in the corridor, holding his new girl. Together, we go in to see his wife. They latch the baby onto her breast, but Gea doesn't take it immediately. Then she does. Gea has latched on, she is eating. A biro trace begins to extend from under her feet: her path, the line that connects her to our irrigation system.

Summer's proper heat seems to arrive suddenly, all in an hour, as Nico and I are leaving the city. The terrace is laden with fruit and flowers, sweating out in the heat. We're all thirsty, and it's not good for the wisteria to be thirsty. Our neighbours and the concierge are entrusted with our aubergines, our tomatoes and our strawberries. They can eat them all if they want.

'Remember that the water pressure changes as people leave the city for the summer. Be careful, even while you're away!' Maria cautions me about the pipes and the spritzers.

I learn that it's good for some of the plants to go thirsty for a while. Who could have thought of that? Walking barefoot on the terrace has become impossible: it's too hot and only the lizards are happy out there. I finish packing my suitcases and leave the flat for the summer.

Nico carries his own suitcases. He no longer needs help to tie his shoes, fall asleep or cut the meat on his plate. He can kill mosquitoes all on his own. Learning these things took him a year, or perhaps only one second. He likes flying, trains, everything except for eating. He has opinions, tastes and unique wishes. He's still asking for a brother. He's still asking when his father and I will get back together. He's also asking whether my new boyfriend should be a kind of second father to him. He asks that my boyfriend and I stay together and never leave him, and whether together we'll make him a brother. He asks his five-year-old girlfriend to make him a thousand children, who I'll have to raise myself because he'll be working as a pilot. He'll be one of those pilots who visits the islands to plant fruit and vegetable orchards. He sleeps well at night and in the morning he says, good morning, Mummy.

'I can't tell if the book I'm writing is working,' I say to Nico.

'Have you put enough of me in it?' he asks. 'The more of me you put in, the better.'

'I've put loads of you in,' I smile. He looks at me seriously.

I look at him seriously.

'Have you put enough planes and trains in there?'

'There are planes and trains,' I say.

'You should put in some tractors and rockets. And a spaceship.'

We land on the island and settle in for the months to come. Every day I send my work out by email before 2 p.m., and the rest of the time we are free to do what we wish. We want to defeat the jellyfish. We want to save planet Earth. We want all children in the world to be able to dive without worry. We must purchase some turtles for the Mediterranean Sea and ask Maria's stumpy tortoise where we might find other turtles like her who are up for visiting us by the seaside. Nico learns to ride a bike without stabilisers, and he becomes a better swimmer. He can take longer walks now. Dive from up high. He is still afraid of big dogs and darkness.

'I don't like being all by myself,' he tells me.

I don't know whether I should substantiate his fear as a foundational aspect of life, or explain that being all by oneself can also mean being free, and so being alone can be a wonderful thing because we're all still connected anyway: wind, traces, biros, swarms, pollen.

My boyfriend and his children join us on the island. We're testing a house, we're testing what it means to be a group, together. We're trying to figure out if two halves of a family make up a new family altogether. We're trying out new subsets, in our infinite garden, and figuring out if a third place that isn't home for any of us might turn out to be the right place for us all. Slowly, I feel myself beginning to wish that my boyfriend's children were mine: when they don't seek my company, I miss them. They won't ever love me wholeheartedly. It hurts, I am jealous, but that's how it is. I feel sorry for Nico sometimes, because he doesn't have a brother, and cannot understand the simple bond of brotherhood between my boyfriend's children.

'I don't like being all by myself,' Nico repeats, once again. 'Sometimes they hit me.'

Sometimes playing family works, sometimes it doesn't. It doesn't work, for instance, when it comes to deciding who sleeps where: Nico is left on his own, and any attempt to convince the other two children to sleep in the same room as him is both sad and unsuccessful. It doesn't work when we project ourselves in the future. Some days I take a walk with them all, secretly hoping people assume they're my children. Bees, pollen, roots. Whenever somebody asks, I keep my answer vague. I come up with phrasing that leaves things open. I love Nico, I love my boyfriend's children, and so I love all children on Earth in the same way. In the swarm, in the forest, I'm hoping all children might see a mother in me. It's not about Nico or my boyfriend's children: no one belongs to me, nor I to them. When my boyfriend and I are out on our own without the kids, and new people ask us how many children we have, I say three. I don't say I have one, and the other two are his. I say three even though it's a lie: we don't even have a single child between us. But if I'm the mother of all children, then I have three, and I also have three billion of them.

'How many children do you have?' people will ask me.

'Three billion,' I'll say.

'Are you well?' my father asks on the phone.

We have taken the kids to the south of the island, and now we're on our way back. The radio is playing tacky, romantic music while the sun sets. Our children say disgusting, hilarious things. We are singing a song by a rapper who wants to make tons of cash. My feet are naked, sand clinging to them. There is salt in my hair. Each time my boyfriend and I look at each other, we smile. We are happy.

'I'm really well,' I say. 'What about you?'

The car is running alongside mountains of salt. The sun is pink, reflecting off the salt crystals. I show my tongue to the children, as if to say: wouldn't it be great to take one big lick off that mountain? Then I frown, as if feeling the bitter taste of the salt on our tongue.

'I'm expecting a baby,' my father says.

'OK,' I say.

My father lists details: number of months, sex. It's a boy. We chat briefly about something else. Then we come back to the baby. My father cracks a few jokes. He calmly explains how the baby won't be a shock to us. He expects this to be true, judging by the way he says it. Shouldn't it have been me to say, I'm expecting a baby? Isn't that how time works?

'It's not important for you anymore,' he adds. 'You don't need me.'

Is it not my turn to have children and a father, like it's the turn of the lizards to lie flat on the terrace enjoying the heat? I could tell my father that there's a difference between developing a habit not to feel need, and real need, in the past and in the present. Or I could just tell him we actually need him.

'Are you happy?' I ask my father.

'Of course,' he says. 'And I think it's a good thing I'm having a baby. My girlfriend is young.'

'And might it be time for us to meet your girlfriend?'

'You think that's necessary?' my father asks.

He sounds sincerely surprised. Or he's a really great actor.

'I'd like to meet her before I meet my new brother, yes. I'd like for those two things not to happen simultaneously.'

'I hadn't thought about that,' he says. Doesn't my father care about his son having sisters and brothers?

I tell my boyfriend that my father is expecting a son and I'm expecting a brother. I'm expecting a brother who'll be almost too young to play with Nico. When my brother is born, Nico will be nearly six. My heart skips a beat, then it goes back to normal. I recognise that skipped beat: it's my heart at four, sixteen, twenty-one years of age. It's my heart as I'll be drawing my last breath. We've left the salt pans long behind. We're reaching the centre of the island. Countryside, olive trees, red earth: the landscape has changed.

'Are you angry?' my boyfriend asks.

I tell him I find it hard to get angry about things like these. Impossible imperatives: love me, desire me – what can one do about them? My boyfriend doesn't understand, he says he'd get angry if it happened to him. I call my brother to see how he's feeling.

'I'm angry,' he says.

I call my sister Diana.

'We should meet his girlfriend,' she agrees. 'I wouldn't want our brother to think we won't be there for him.'

I don't call Allegra yet. She's been living in New Zealand for thirteen years, and I still can't remember the time difference.

At night, in bed, I run my own calculations again. When my brother is Nico's age, his father will be almost seventy. What's it like for a child to encounter old age so early in life? To find out about decay instead of strength? And my father, once more a father, won't be a grandfather to our children, nor to his young son's offspring. So in one respect, as far as grandparents go, my new brother's children will be sharing the same fate as Nico. The only difference for them will be the certainty of my father's absence, which will imply an absence of expectations. My father wasn't a father. Now he won't be a grandfather. Or conversely: will he finally be a father, now he is becoming a father again? Going through parenthood at sixty seems so tiring, though I suppose it could also be exciting, like a real-life simulation of starting from scratch. Starting again, though, means repeating things when one is no longer young, and less strong, and less fresh. I don't hold a moral judgement on the matter, but isn't it like playing the same videogame level repeatedly, running into the same monsters and pitfalls as level one, instead of moving forward through the game?

Being sixty and dealing with the monsters and pitfalls of being sixty seems to me like a much more complicated task. Perhaps at sixty, or seventy, one might want to start thinking about what kind of life they are leaving behind, instead of spending time at nursery school, or teaching somebody their table manners – yes, thank you, goodnight – or second languages, finding money for second language courses without a lot of money to spare. What does a seventy-year-old father think about smoking weed? How about cigarettes? His life is about to end, in ten or twenty years. I call my mother to figure out how she feels.

'I thought it'd hurt less,' she says. 'I feel even more lonely.'

She practically raised us as a single mother. Now she's a single grandparent. But I think what really hurts her is the subterranean conviction that she still had more time to fix things, even to get back together. When something as massive as this happens, some convictions become less credible. In a positive sense, it also interrupts certain loops.

'How can he want a small child now?' she asks. 'Won't his back hurt? Won't he get bored?'

In a way, a small child is always a marvel, I think. It's just that I wonder if it wouldn't be easier to follow a natural pace, like the plants, summer and the passing of time. My father could walk alongside us, his grown children, eat with us, talk to us as peers, without ever having to strain his back. He could pass down his experience of past marriages and time, being thirty, forty and fifty. He could fill his grown children with his memories, his present, and listen to their lives. Spend time with them. I mean, with us.

I am sad that a boy is coming into the world already alone, like we were. But my brother will be alone, as we've all been alone, whatever way we put it. I imagine the flat that this baby will grow up in, with an absent, old father and a young woman who will feel abandoned. When I pick up a newborn baby at my age, resting them against my breast, I certainly feel physically and mentally like a mother, rather than a sister. When it picks up a baby, my body is thinking feed, not play. Summer. Winter.

'When do we become adults?' Nico would ask.

After that night I don't think about my brother a great deal, but I find I blurt it out unexpectedly to people. 'I'm expecting a brother,' I say. Or: 'My father is expecting a son.' People's reactions range from indifference to disappointment. Only my husband texts back, How amazing. I don't even know where he's texting me from, and when I receive his message, I'm no longer sure why I told him about my father's baby in the first place.

When I come back from the island I also come back to my life with Nico. We're older, better adjusted and stronger. The lemon tree has put out tens of lemons. The fig tree has wide leaves and hangs heavy with fruit. I am now missing my boyfriend's kids, as well as him, and I'm nervous about spending another winter alone in this flat, watching the plants turn red, then yellow, then still. Taking Nico to school in the morning. Taking Nico to the pool, to his English classes. Being cold. Not hugging. I'm wondering whether I should grow new plants, put down more intelligent roots, or not. Should I accept that solitude is my new truth, or go out and mingle with others again? Fix the doors because they're unsafe, or leave the weak locks in place since I might move again to a different house, city and life? Nico and I are stronger, but also weaker, because we are alone again. We are alone every time I forget I'm the mother of three billion children on Earth. Thinking about it, I should look after my three billion children better: I keep saying I'll do it, but then I never do. What about the vegetable workshop on my terrace? To try to tidy up my thoughts and my present, I start taking ever more notes. I arrange the sentences, divide the material in sets and in subsets. I write a synopsis. I move some pots around, set a year, a plot, hammer in some nails to help the ramblers climb, and I map out the blank pages with a biro. They multiply.

The Shape of Life

'I didn't want to wake you,' says the psychic, tapping on my forehead.

'Then why are you tapping on my forehead?' I ask.

'To make you sleep better,' she smiles. 'And because I want to remind you that you're in the present. You're alive, you're well. You are here. The blackbird is already your friend, and you are already writing.'

I close my eyes. I see the blackbird. I open them again. I see my father.

The psychic keeps tapping. I synchronise my breathing with hers. I synchronise my heart to her heart. She taps louder. I breathe louder.

'Sleep again,' she says. 'Deeper now. As if you were dead.'

'Hold it,' I say. 'I really don't fancy death.'

'And you think you're unique in that?'

She increases the pressure of her fingers, their pace, and I fall asleep. Maybe I nearly die.

We are at my mother's gallery – my grandfather's former factory. Our literary festival is on, the one named after the totemic machine, which now takes place in the absence of the totemic machine. We are sitting in the courtyard and Mr Bharat is here too; he has come to Italy especially for us, before pursuing more printing machines elsewhere. It's a muted year for the festival: there are fewer people, fewer lights. Less to eat and to drink. Maybe this has something to do with the absence of the Roland Ultra too: we miss it; does it miss us? I no longer feel like I know my husband, he is far away. I've never known my father, he's always been away. My new boyfriend also lives far away, will I ever know him? The blackbird is gradually getting closer, but it will never come close enough. It will never land on Nico's shoulders, as he wishes it would. It will never help us tidy up after dinner.

'I just wanted to know how the machine is doing,' I ask Mr Bharat. 'Can you tell me what happened once you got to India?'

Mr Bharat smiles and says the Roland is doing well: it's printing boxes, it keeps people in work and it's a very beautiful object. And so I imagine the machine, more handsome than ever, making work for people, making boxes in a tropical Indian jungle full of elephants, tigers, monkeys and other animals. There's a cheetah. There's a peacock. I picture various monkeys and bison. Later that night I send an email to my father.

Dear Dad,
We have missed you all our lives. I just wanted to tell you

in case you were wondering whether we'd noticed your absence. It's a pity you've been around so little. How come that, when you and Mum broke up, you never considered we could stay at yours, or suggested at least having dinner once a week with your children? Twice every five years? Once every ten? Why didn't you ever spend a weekend with us? Take us on trip? If I hadn't been sending you emails, would we have kept in touch at all, you and I? Don't you like being a father and a grandfather? When you told me you were expecting a child, you said, 'You no longer need me. It can't be a shock,' as if you had to explain that to me – you said it as an imperative. You decided it. You weren't here when we needed you; we need you now, and you're not here. It made me sad at fifteen, at twenty-two, and now I'm thirty-five, it still makes me sad. I'm sorry if these words hurt your feelings but I think it's important not to keep them to myself. Perhaps it's because I hope that your story won't repeat itself. This isn't an accusation, nor is it a judgement: it's *your* story, after all. But I needed to tell you – and by doing so, I'm also telling you something about myself. Hugs to you, Anna

That same night, he replies.

Dear Anna,
So you're writing a book again. How can I help you as your father – not as a reader, a lawyer or judge – in this new cruel, half-plausible retelling? Every father is one of their own kind, and that can't be changed – this is the core of your frustration, I believe (a lack of patience). Like many

other things in life (perhaps all of them?), we must accept the whole parcel. And like many other things in life (all of them?), circumstances tend to change as your position in time changes. I'd divide our life at least into two parts: you four, as children, you as grown-ups. You four, grown up, are not my life, and the story of our faraway past needn't be thought of as completely straightforward. My life and my love have been a little autistic perhaps, but I've always been like that, since my very first memory, when I was as young as your niece Gea, up until the present day. Seeing my children grown up has been an immense surprise: I've felt happiness and relief in seeing you all become people – autonomous, independent – as if a miraculous task was accomplished at the very time our family life fell apart. Those two things happened simultaneously: they ripened together. So isn't it all too easy to remind me about the dinners and holidays I have supposedly missed, when all my life I've eschewed dinners and a social life? Isn't this a fruit of your own narrative cruelty? We represent characters in the way that we see them from the standpoint of our own perspective: you do it; me, likewise. Let's cut to the chase: you've had a blind father, sane of mind, with an average personality, but blind. If you think about it, his blindness irritates you: 'For fuck's sake! Look out for that pole you're about to walk into! Jesus Christ, how are you not enjoying that wonderful rainbow?' This is why you resent me: you don't want to be in the category of the world I can't see. You don't think that blindness applies to family: look at us! Love us! Roles must be written with rigour and care. The clothes you have me wear in your script aren't my own. My absence is biological, it means being there when it's needed, instantly and surprisingly, and soon no longer: this is the shape of life, what we were born for. Your thoughts about me now, in short, are good practice for when I'll no longer be around. My certainty is that there was a time in my life in which I enjoyed a deep, intense and mutual love with the people who surrounded me (you don't need to agree with this, though it involves you – it is my own feeling, from when you were small and thin as a reed, climbing all over me and hugging me). My hope is I'll be granted another period like that, again, sometimes, with everyone who matters to me. To me, a blind man, that's enough. Bye, Dad

We don't write again, and as usual we don't see each other either. I know the map of this distance too well to welcome it as something new or wish to explore it again.

Maria comes back from America and she's happy. She tells me about the hospital and the horticultural therapy gardens. There are green areas reserved for children or mental health patients. She tells me about taking neighbourhood walks with the volunteers, easy paths that can be completed in fifteen minutes, walking slowly.

'There's nothing specifically therapeutic or special about the walks themselves. They're just walks. Of course, you're stimulating touch, smell and language. You can talk about plants, if you want, but it's meant more as a conversation starter.' She tells me that her supervisor's hair was as crazy as it looked in the picture we'd seen on the internet. She tells me about the workshops she ran with children, terminal patients, people bowled over by chemotherapy: 'They're all open workshops, except the one with the burn patients. I've seen two serious burn victims – both had lost an arm – building a birdhouse together for the local sparrows and bats. One was holding the wood as the other used the hammer.' She tells me that this system really helps when one is in hospital, feeling completely lost. For instance, she met two parents whose son had been brought into hospital only twenty-four hours earlier. They were distraught, but joining the burn victim group really helped them to feel grounded in a familiar, intelligible space. 'Group activities don't last very long. Ten, fifteen minutes,' she says. 'They help the relatives cope, not only during an immediate emergency, but later, particularly when someone has to stay in hospital for a very long time. In the winter, when it gets too cold to work outside in the garden, they bring their work inside, in front of the windows. Seasons keep changing out there. The hospital garden keeps on existing, its leaves protecting and propagating life on the outside.'

I make her lunch and we open the doors to the terrace and walk out together. The garden keeps on existing; the lizards, somewhere, are waiting.

We Will Be Forest!

Gea – my mother's gallery, my grandfather's former factory, the place where Maria had her aneurysm and my brother held his wedding – is having a big opening party for the Roland Ultra exhibit. Nico roams the rooms taking photos on my smartphone. The noises of Delhi play out in a dark room, where a small torch sheds light in the dusty corners. Nathalie du Pasquier's drawings, representing the Roland as a sacred Indian cow, hang in a small glass case. Large-size videos are projecting images of Indian roads, and of the machine working at full steam. The walls of Gea are covered in photographs.

In the main room, where the Roland used to be bolted down, there's a hanging net, on which an image of the machine is projected. The Roland Ultra becomes a lingering ghost. There's music. There are fruit boxes printed in India. My boyfriend, who is passing through Milan, buys the large print of a roof, on which a dog and a man are walking, towering over the slums and the plants. In the photograph, the green of the plants has swallowed up the buildings, and the balcony appears like a launchpad stretching out over nature: a new perspective on green, leaves and the top of the houses, from far above other people's hearts and heads. I imagine taking care of my garden until its leaves and plants swallow everything up: us, other people, the landscape. Then we will all live in a forest, we will all be forest, together with parrots and lizards, and kangaroos, and it will be humankind this time around who'll bring back the wilderness.

That evening, my husband and his new girlfriend come to Gea too. We say hello. Serena has shaved her head for a show. She's very beautiful and suddenly seems taller. Are you a sunflower too? I try to talk to her in Spanish. She says I speak it quite well. I watch her play with Nico, and my heart gathers speed, but then, rapidly, it settles again. She and my husband leave. We stay about an hour longer, and as we're taking Nico home the sky is full of bright stars that we are able to see, and not full of stars we can't see.

'Since when can you see stars from here?' my boyfriend asks.

I smile at him, as if I could take credit for it: as if I'd put the stars up there in the sky to make him understand that, when we're together, when we are near, even the city fills up with them. The wind is blowing. The air smells like countryside earth.

'It's definitely thanks to us that you can see the stars tonight,' I suggest.

We get home and I put Nico to bed. I join my boyfriend

in the kitchen and, as usual, there's very little in the fridge. Nico eats very little. By this point, I, too, prefer to survive on almonds, and in any case, I could be standing in the middle of the Indian forest, and there still wouldn't be enough plants for me. We pour ourselves a glass of wine and step out to look at the stars again. We hug.

'When are you moving to London?' he asks.

'You could move to Milan,' I say.

'Do you want me to move to Milan?'

'I want to come where you are, and for you to come to me,' I say. 'Forever.'

The stars spell out W-O-W on the vault of the sky.

'I plan to start moving the plants soon. We have to shift around some weights, rebalance things,' Maria says on the phone the following morning. 'You should check how much weight your terrace is able to withstand.'

'I'd love to have some trees, actually,' I say.

'You can't have them; their roots are too large.'

'Do you mean I'm the kind of person who isn't able to put down roots?'

'I'm talking about the terrace. It'll collapse if you put trees out there.'

'Not even a single tree?'

'Not there, no.' I can't have trees here! When am I moving to London?

Maria comes round to work out the new plant arrangement, bringing along an assistant because they've become too big. The two of them walk around the terrace, and along the communal walkways. Some of the pots won't fare well much longer up here, so we'll have to move them down to the courtyard, for everyone to enjoy. I like growing plants I can share with others. Trees. Children. I could plant whole woods beginning today. I could change the air we breathe, and the notions of family, of home. I explained this to Nico a few months ago, but perhaps back then I didn't fully believe it. He already thinks of home as the movement between two different houses. Did I lie to Nico when I asked him to trust me, to believe that the corridors of our home stretched out in the open air? Now I can believe that too.

'Why does my father get to have twelve trees and I can't even have one?' I ask Maria.

'Is this a question that really requires an answer?' Her assistant looks on with pity. Or maybe he likes me. He likes me and he pities me at the same time.

'He also has five children,' I whisper, so no one can hear me. 'I only have one.' When the assistant leaves, I tell Maria: 'I reckon my father will end up with seven kids. Seventeen, even.'

'I've started seeing somebody new,' she interrupts me.

'We're very different. He doesn't understand much of what I tell him, and I don't understand much of what he tells me. He doesn't know anything about plants. He is fussy about mud and animals. He doesn't even like my tortoise. But I like him. I like him a lot.' After lunch, Maria eradicates the dead sunflowers. She chops off their heads, retrieving the seeds inside. 'I'm only taking out a few – Nico can do the rest. You should put the seeds out to dry, so you can feed them to the birds, who will help us disseminate them.'

When Nico comes back from school, I show him how to do it, and he is very keen on the idea. Over the following days, we lay the sunflowers out to dry and start stripping their seeds. Nico and my boyfriend have produced bird feed: a magic act. Now we know how to keep a living being well fed. And birds know how to help us disseminate the seeds.

'The first seeds are for the blackbird,' Nico says.

'They're for all the birds,' I say.

'They're for all the birds who want to live here,' he specifies. 'We can't pick favourites.'

I'm the mother of three billion children, I can't choose to feed a single blackbird. In the morning we put out a bird house full of sunflower seeds, for the blackbird, and the other four hundred billion birds who inhabit the planet. For a few days, the seeds just sit there, and nobody eats them. Not the blackbird, nor the pigeons. Each time we come home we feel a little worried. Nico is upset.

'Let's move our house,' he tells me one day.

'Our house?' I say brightly.

'The blackbird's house. We can't move our house.'

'You pick where,' I suggest. Nico moves the blackbird's house further away.

'The blackbird needs to be further away from us, to be able to eat,' he explains.

From the kitchen, we watch the little bird house at the bottom of the terrace. It's a little white triangle: a concept, right down to its shape. The following day, the blackbird starts eating, and we have breakfast listening to the singing birds.

'Let's move it closer now,' Nico says. 'Slowly slowly.'

So every day Nico moves the bird house closer by a few centimetres. Every day, he plucks new seeds from the sunflowers, and the blackbird continues eating them. Eventually, the bird house is too close to our house again, and so the blackbird stops coming.

'It has to be far enough,' Nico says. 'That's how we find the right distance.'

The Roland Ultra exhibit stays open for a few more months. It hosts book launches and a couple of private parties. At the closing event, there are more celebrations, Indian snacks and cups of bancha tea.

My mother tells me they only sold three prints. Nico goes over to the video of the Roland printing in India, holding my smartphone to take a video of the video. He asks people if he can take their portrait. He takes pictures of the curried lentils. All the photographs are taken from below, from his perspective. In his images, the world is full of giant people and sky. There's me sitting on a bench, and Mr Bharat. There's my sister Diana and my brother with his wife, holding their baby girl, Gea. Around us, both in shot and outside, is the whole planet.

'I want to leave,' I tell my mother. It's a revelation to say it out loud, first and foremost, for me.

'Come on, stay at least until the end of the party.'

'I mean I want to leave this city.'

'You can't,' she says. 'What will Nico and his dad do?'

'I want to go to a place that's at the right distance. Things would change, but not that much really. I'd take Nico here four days a month, and his father could visit for four days. Or it could be five and five. Anything's possible, basically.'

'You can't,' she repeats. 'Nico is happy here.'

'He's happy. Here. There. He's happy, in general, and he'll continue being happy. I'd like to live with my boyfriend. I want to leave this city. Grow trees. I could have more children. I could have six more. Nine, if I put in the effort.'

'Do you want nine more children?'

By this point, we could laugh or get angry. Since I'm not sure how I feel, I focus on my breath, as I've been taught to do in my antenatal classes, in yoga and by apps that I use on my iPhone when I feel nervous about flying. I've been taught to breathe like this so many times, by so many different voices and whispers. I relax my diaphragm. I rehearse the whispers. Is learning to breathe a pointless endeavour, like believing you can train your heart to beat in the way you prefer? How can I think I'll be able to decide which sunflower grows the tallest?

'You'll find a way,' my mother tells me.

'But I don't feel like I'm actually in any one place, living like this. I'm not loving anyone properly.'

'Aren't you the one who keeps saying everything's in movement? What's that word you like to use? Swarm.'

'We wouldn't be talking about this if I were moving one hour away by train. Are you scared of flying?'

'That's you. Do you still want that dog, by the way?'

I bring it up with my husband too. For months, I try to put into words the reason why leaving is the right thing to do. I even bring up the dog. We could co-own it, it could follow Nico to whichever house Nico goes to. Fortunately, my husband says no to the dog. I come up with a thousand different versions of why I should leave. He always says no. Sometimes I'm in Milan with Nico while my husband is away for work, and that makes me angry. I get angry if I'm in Milan with Nico and my husband doesn't make an effort to see him. But I know that my plan won't work without my husband's help: I need his help to explain to Nico that our home keeps becoming bigger and bigger, that the main corridor that joins our room now includes several airports, and that the Alps are now sitting in our living room.

'I read that Virginia Woolf went to lots of parties. You lied to me!' I shout to my mother.

'They were different parties. More intellectual. And she begrudged going,' my mother says.

The exhibition is dismantled, and the photographs wrapped up. The room is empty again. I go to see the packed-up photos with Nico, and we zoom through each room on his scooter. Gea is no longer an art gallery – it is again my grandfather's former factory. The art goes and the Indians leave. My mother wants to sell the factory. No Ping. No Pong.

My mother asks me if I'd want to take the plants in the courtyard home for myself.

'Shall we put down the new plants?' Maria asks on the phone as I roam the empty three thousand square metres of the factory, in the darkness.

'No,' I say. She's taken aback. 'OK, let's do it,' I immediately correct myself.

'Are you sure?' Maria asks again.

'Sure,' I confirm.

Nothing bad can come from more seeds and more flowers. Even if I do leave, if I do manage to convince everybody, and will never own a dog, the forest will keep growing. It will reach me anywhere – certainly in my new house – and the distance won't matter. We'll share the same habitat. Eat the same fruit. We'll be protected, like butterflies. We'll swing from tree to tree holding onto the same liana. Or our monkeys will do that. We'll plant new plants and weeds, new moving things: wild, strong and fast-growing. Plants that can hide and protect us. We'll create a moving picture in which distance will be undetectable, and therefore non-existent. I will bury Milan under a thick wood of trees. I'll bury the void and turn it into flowers, fruits and greenery. Crocodiles will come, but we won't be afraid of them, because we'll be the ones who gave them a place to live. A forest, from here to London. Our forest. No room for the void between me and the world. Only trees, roots, good chemistry.

As I roam the empty factory with Nico, I find a photographic book about the preparation of the Roland Ultra for its long overseas trip. A few pages in, I notice a photograph I hadn't encountered before. It's Alessandro, on the day that the dismantling work began. I'd forgotten he'd been here. I'd forgotten about him.

Alessandro and Diana tell each other they miss being together, or that they don't miss it; one day they're fighting, the next they're OK. Diana has found a flat to buy; it's very small, but it has a balcony. Alessandro, too, has found a new home. They have bought two separate houses. They've organised them; they've chosen new kitchens and new shelves. They're kissing new people, planning trips without consulting each other, and this would be the case even if they chose to travel to the Philippines. They're cooking for others and sometimes they are so far apart, for so many months, that they no longer know anything about the other. As work begins on her new flat, my sister tells me: 'I wonder if the builders think that my father is dead, since he never comes to visit or give me advice.' I imagine my father dead. I imagine his funeral. I pick the song 'Absolute Beginners' to play because he taught us to sing it as kids. The fact that Diana thinks that our father is on the builders' mind as much as he is on hers makes me smile. Does Diana ever think about the builders' dads?

'It's not like I'm married to this place because I own the flat,' Diana says, as soon as the house is ready.

'Of course,' I say. 'If I were you, I'd start emptying it.'

Touch as Many Things as You Can

Around Christmas time, I leave with Nico, my boyfriend and his children again. We spend a week together and we are happy. We spend time, as usual, in a third place that isn't my home or theirs. It is a simple place where nobody has a past or is expected to organise the future. We can be good, here, in the awareness that all things end. We can make up new rules and new pleasures, so long as they last a finite amount of time. Nobody's expected to go shopping for groceries or fix the front door or arrange paediatric care. It's very easy to love each other in a place where we don't own anything, and nothing is demanding to be fixed. We can be kind to each other here because we know we will only have to be kind for a week. We can be sweet because nobody will need to look after us later, in our bitterness and fatigue, long after the holiday has ended and all the things we can't do and must do begin afresh. When flu strikes us down in the winter, we will all be far away from each other again, but out here we are strong and tanned. Out here we understand nature: we let it be, we let each other be. I don't smile often when I'm at home, but when I'm here, I am always smiling.

One evening we're sitting in a restaurant when I receive an email from my father.

Romeo was born this evening, a couple of weeks earlier than we expected. He seems beautiful to me, and good – perhaps he will be this way for the rest of his life. On this long day everything went to plan, so I'm going to bed tired, happy and under attack from my own brain. Bye, Dad

Bye. Where I'm on holiday, it looks like summer. It's the middle of winter where my father is. I reread the email a couple of times. I receive seven others, with pictures attached. In some of the pictures, the baby boy – my brother – is in his cot alone. In some, my father is holding him in his arms. In one, he is feeding his son with a bottle.

'I've just had a brother,' I tell the children.

'What do you mean, your brother?' they ask. They don't remember they were by my side when I first found out about the pregnancy.

'Who are his parents?' Nico asks.

'Grandad,' I say.

'Your grandad? Who's your grandad?' the children all ask simultaneously.

'It's your father's. I mean: he's my father's. Your grandad's son.'

'But he's old! Can he do that?' Nico asks.

'He can do that.'

'But he'll die if he's old,' he says.

Then I don't say anything, because I'm the kind of person who has trouble admitting a mother could die in a fairy tale, let alone a real mother or father in real life. Certainly, what's happening to me isn't easy to digest for the children: now they wonder if they'll have another brother – meanwhile, I've acquired a sort of stepmother. I'd like to tell Nico there is no time limit on acquiring a sibling. But I don't.

'Who's his mum?' the children ask.

'My father's girlfriend. I've never met her,' I explain.

Nico begins doodling on his napkin. Everyone is quickly distracted. I go through the pictures again, looking at the sheets in which my brother sleeps. The bedding has the same motif as the bedding at the hospital where Nico was born: Dalmatian puppies. Do I want a little puppy? I am wondering if, miraculously, this is really the same set of sheets they wrapped Nico in. Dalmatian puppies upon which Nico was laid, as soon as he exited my body; Dalmatian puppies on which my new brother now rests. The same coffee cups I use at the bar, which my ex-husband uses next. Boxes labelled 'books', 'my clothes' and 'your clothes'.

'How are you feeling?' my boyfriend asks.

'I'm not feeling,' I say.

'Then write,' he says, copying my mother.

My mother goes back to India to be away from everything, including my father's new baby – our brother. My sister Allegra joins her there from New Zealand and together they undertake a strict Panchakarma regime. I'm not sure what Panchakarma is, so I look it up on Google. I read that Panchakarma is an ancient Ayurvedic cleansing practice, which employs herbs and natural oils to purify the body. According to Ayurveda, a person is in good health when his body and soul are in perfect alignment with nature. Due to an incorrect lifestyle, many individuals suffer illnesses that are due to worsen in time. It is possible, on the other hand, to re-establish a balance to the dosha – the three biological principles that rule all living beings – aiming for a better, happier existence.

When they're done with the Panchakarma routine, my mother and Allegra send us pictures in which they both look beautiful and relaxed. Their hair is shiny. Their teeth are very white and there's a glow to their skin. They smile like people in India. They're sitting on a cliff. They're walking in the city. They're wrapped up in saris. Then my sister goes back to New Zealand and my mother stays behind, in India. Initially, my mother says she wants to come back to Italy; she calls me to tell me she is feeling nostalgic. I tell her it is raining here. Real bad weather. It's grim when it doesn't rain, let alone when it does! Don't come back!

'But I miss you,' she explains. 'I miss you, and bad weather, or rain, doesn't change that. I don't care about that.'

'Would you want to come back if the sky was pouring with radioactive rain, or if we lived in a city ravaged simultaneously by an earthquake and a volcanic explosion?'

'Silly billy,' my mother says.

'You didn't answer my question,' I say.

She stays longer in India. She sends me pictures of the sunrise. She sends us a few emails saying she is well. Two more weeks go by.

Dear loves,

Today I'm going to visit an architect's studio in Mumbai. It's an hour away by boat plus an hour south by car, so I'm staying overnight. Tomorrow I'm going to Ahmedabad for a wedding that will last for four days. I should've probably done the Panchakarma cure and all the rest of it *after*, and not before, this long trip, but I couldn't have done it with Allegra that way, and her presence was such a gift to me. We laughed so much together. I'm full of luggage, carrying the usual silly Indian presents for the children, and it's a little unwieldy to travel this way, but still, it's so good to be on the road again! I love being in movement. Yesterday I spent the day with a girl I met last year who is getting married in February. I can't stick out here that long unfortunately, so she wanted to show me where the function will take place and she also invited me to the tasting session for one of the nine different buffets that will be held, along with some of her family members and her in-laws, who she'll live with after the wedding, as tradition dictates. It was a very fun day: everyone was saying what worked and what didn't, suggesting that salt or sugar should be added to the dish, or mint swapped for basil, that the meatballs should be a different shape. The chefs and the organisers listened diligently, respectfully taking notes. Everything will be vegetarian, and cooked differently for the Jainist guests, who don't eat garlic, onion, potato and aubergine, and don't drink alcohol. Right now, there's a beautiful sunrise spreading over the sea, complete with seagulls and rocking boats. Very romantic, like in a 1950s American movie. Lots of kisses and I'll see you soon. Your Mum

A 1950s American movie – like Alessandro's visions during his chemical coma. Alessandro has told me that he only felt pain for forty-eight hours during the entirety of his rehabilitation and surgery after the incident. The painful days were those that followed the operation on his wrist. Once he got home, his physical rehabilitation began with small movements of the fingers.

'Touch as many things as you can,' his physiotherapist told him. 'The brain is great at forgetting, but it really struggles to remember things.'

Holding an object between two fingers was at first an impossible task for him. The biggest hurdle was thin objects – anything light, with an edge. A bit like Maria, who for months, after spending so long in bed, felt proud even just getting up in the morning, and began to think she had fully healed once she was capable of making the bed.

'I couldn't feel a thing to begin with,' Alessandro has told me. 'I'd lost my sense of touch completely. I'd go to this specialist centre where a woman would massage my tendons for thirty minutes. Her massage was so gentle I couldn't even feel it. Sometimes she'd tell me, "This will hurt a bit," and then she would hurt me. Even then, I was only a body, and being a body was sweet, comfortable for the mind.'

There are people on Earth who know the very last thing about the functioning of a hand. Of a single finger. Other people know everything about fingernails. This kind of hyper-specialised knowledge must be similar to having a very clear mission in life, and it helps in retaining the names of important small things that must be kept in existence: fingernails, seeds, ourselves. Cherry laurels. Nico.

'Touch as many things as you can,' I tell myself.

I repeat to myself that the brain is great at forgetting. In the same way as I've learnt to forget about my life with my husband: our love, intimacy, knowledge. Is there a reason why the brain works this way? 'Touch as many things as you can,' I tell myself once more, and finally allow myself to imagine that touching as many things as possible could be a rule that applies to most things in life. To my husband and me. To myself and my father, who finds that the memory of me climbing onto him at age four is all that he needs. This may well be the best teaching I can offer Nico, though children are typically taught to do the opposite: don't touch this, don't touch that. It would make more sense to tell Nico to touch as many things as he can. To get marks on his hands, to get dirty: write, create, be forest.

'Put your hand on my head,' Nico says in bed.

'What do you mean?'

'Like a hat for the cold,' he says, as if it were obvious. Touch me. Make me exist. If you don't kiss me, I dies.

How Are Your Plants Getting On?

Nico and I decide to visit my brother. We want to touch him. We bring a few clothes from when Nico was a baby, a few toys from the past and now for the future, and a greetings card I've asked Nico to draw. Nico writes 'Romeo' on it, which is the name of my brother. As we walk to my father's place together, we are both grown-ups. Even Nico is a grown-up, now he knows how to write 'Romeo'.

'Am I his uncle, then?'

'He's your uncle,' I explain on the tram.

'But I can hold him. I'm the uncle.'

'That's fine by me,' I say.

'Who are you, then?'

'His sister.'

'What else?'

'Whatever you prefer.'

Outside, the city is the same one I was born in, the same one Nico was born in, the same as it was a few weeks ago, when Romeo was born. We arrive at our destination, and the building is the same one that hosted my parents' publishing house. We climb up the five floors, and though it is Saturday, the office that has replaced the publishers is open. I read on the bronze plaque that it is a lawyers' firm. Inside, I recognise some of the furniture from my past, thrown in together with objects from their present: a new reception desk, different lighting. There are no books. And I'm no longer there.

'This used to be your grandparents' office,' I tell Nico.

'Which grandparents? Mine?'

'Look, it doesn't matter.'

I don't have to explain every single little thing to him. At some point, Nico will become interested in his own past himself; he'll explore backwards and forwards and think, look at this, look at that, that's the way it used to be.

We reach the fifth floor and my father and his girlfriend welcome us in. She has kind eyes. Long legs. The living room hosts half of my father's office. Instead of moving himself, he has moved what was left of his work in here. In the middle of the living room is the cot, and in the cot is my brother, asleep. My sister Allegra began life in a similar way: in a cot in the middle of the tiny room of a publishing house run by my twenty-five-year-old mother and father. I look at my brother.

'*Che bel visin*,' I say.

The grandmother in me has a ridiculous accent. And dentures. Cataracts. Lots of rings.

My father sits down in the corridor to play with Nico's toy cars. I chat to his girlfriend. We talk about my brother.

We exchange motherly advice traded down from our grandmothers.

'Is he eating good?' I ask.

My father's girlfriend nods. She says my father is a wonderful father: sometimes she goes out in the evening, and she leaves him to look after the baby. When she comes back, she sometimes finds him a little stressed, but overall my father is really a wonderful father. I don't ask if it's my father or the baby who gets stressed. We go to the kitchen and my father gives Nico a can of Coke. You can see their terrace from the kitchen.

'How are your plants getting on?' I ask my father's girlfriend.

'I'm not sure,' she says. 'I've only just moved in. I arrived the day before Romeo was born.'

'I know that the apricot tree was sick.'

'Was it?' she says.

I look out, and though I am trying, I am still unable to tell what illness looks like in an apricot tree. My father's girlfriend doesn't say a thing. Not that I'm making compelling conversation myself. We go back to talking about babies: rules, naps, opinions on vaccines.

'Now you are four...' my father, the wonderful father, says to Nico, in the corridor.

'I'm five and a half,' Nico corrects him.

'Right, so I said,' says my father, the wonderful father. 'Now we have to hang out more often, so we can race our toy cars.'

'All right,' says Nico.

I hope this is true, because I can bear anything except a

promise like this going unmet. And well, Coca-Cola to my kid? I'd rather not. We stay for another twenty minutes. My brother remains asleep, and I touch his hands. His closed eyes look like tiny seeds. I look at him again and bid him welcome, without speaking. What colour is your biro? How tall will you grow, and in which pot?

Nico and I say a proper goodbye to my father and his girl-friend and skip down the five floors back to the street. We have been very quick. We've been with them, and it's like we weren't. It is only us two again. And we can both walk very well.

'I'll have four children, or maybe a thousand, and you'll look after them all,' Nico repeats.

'But they'll want you.'

'I'll have to work,' Nico says. 'I'll be a pilot, a waiter and a hotel manager. If you come to my hotel, I won't make you pay, and I'll put you up in an all-gold room.'

'Must be cold sleeping in gold bedsheets.'

'Not in my hotel,' Nico says. 'Or I'll be a farmer, so you won't have to do the shopping.'

Whatever plans he is making, Nico factors me in. He wants to take care of me. He wants me to sleep in gold bedsheets. He wants me not to worry about doing the shopping. Sometimes he wants to be a policeman so he can make sure I'll never get fined.

There are two people fighting and screaming in the street. They swear a lot, they shout 'get the fuck out of here or I'll kill you' through their teeth.

'I wonder what happened,' I say to Nico.

'Maybe they're a couple,' he says.

It's two men fighting, both around sixty, driving two separate cars, but this is Nico's interpretation of the scene. I'm almost certain he only saw me and his father argue twice, and we definitely didn't scream swear words or 'I'll kill you' at each other.

I meet up with Alessandro and he tells me he is expecting a baby with his new girlfriend Luisa. The baby is a boy, and he'll be born soon. They've almost finished getting the house ready.

'Maybe it's the wrong flat for a baby,' he says, 'but it'll have to do for some time.' Babies, houses, boxes. 'I'm more of a grown-up these days.'

'So, how do you know when you've become an adult?' Nico would ask him.

'I've started writing. I'm writing about you, and us – is that OK?' I ask Alessandro instead.

'I have no problem with getting attention,' he smiles.

Less than two years have passed, and now Alessandro's hands are capable of holding objects, even the smallest ones, and he has a girlfriend and a baby on the way. His son is coming, also for me. He'll be son three-billion-and-one. Maria has a new boyfriend: she is travelling, and her fear is finally dissipating. Her hair is long again, and she has left behind healthy grain, branches and flowers wherever she's been. My terrace overflows with greenery, it is loaded, ready: the forest is here, and everywhere.

'I'm sending you the manuscript I've been working on,' I tell Maria. 'It's about you, and us.' She is anxious, afraid.

'Read it in your own time. If you don't like it, I'll delete the whole story.'

I send her the initial few chapters and she takes a long time to call me back.

'I've taken a while to reply because I received some test results as I was reading. They weren't good, so I couldn't continue to read. I kept thinking that this story – yours, too, as well as mine – must have a happy ending. I couldn't believe I was reading about this marathon of change, which taught us some simple, healthy facts about our lives, and then, when I reached the end, you'd have to write I was sick again.'

'And how are you doing?' I ask. I'm scared.

'The test results were fine.' I can hear her smile. 'I'm calling to confirm that, for now, your book can have a happy ending. When are we hanging out? It's not raining tomorrow, right?'

We're in Bloom

I take Nico to my ex-husband's house, and I find that the avocado tree has grown immensely. It's green. Lustrous and smooth. My ex-husband's girlfriend says hi. She's also lustrous and smooth. Their house is made up of their avocado tree: it is their ceiling, their identity.

'How's the avocado tree doing?' I ask.

'Really well, thanks,' says my ex-husband.

He says it in an arrogant way and so I feel envy. Nico takes the water spritzer and starts cleaning the leaves of the avocado tree. I could steal the avocado tree: kidnap it and ask for ransom. I could turn it into a massive tree at mine, on my own terrace. Then my terrace would collapse. Just one of the usual things I like to imagine.

'How do you look after an avocado tree?'

'My girlfriend is good with plants.'

Before I leave, I make a small dent in a leaf with my fingernail. The leaf knows that I know.

Maria comes to visit my terrace and the plants have grown so big that it's time to make decisions about them. This isn't just because of their size, and that there are so many, but also because we are ready to give them away. To begin with, I'd like to take over the communal stairwell and the courtyard.

'I'd like to colonise the stairs and the courtyard,' I say.

'I know what you mean,' Maria smiles. She says it as if it had always been her grand plan, and I am merely the newest recruit in her army. We plan out a strategy together, thinking about which plants we will move, and which we will need to relocate away from the terrace. Maria tells me which plants I will have to part with, even if I'm not feeling like it.

'You can't let them grow bigger out here. You need to let them go.'

So, we make choices. We let things go. We make an agreement about the date she will come, with her strong male assistant, to take care of it all. That evening, in London, I receive a letter from her.

Anna,

There were three of us round yours today, because Pino, the man who'd agreed to help me, had a bad back, so he brought along another kid – though in the end they both helped out with things. We separated and repotted the photinia, the laurel, the mulberry and the bay tree. We dismantled and rebuilt the rocky trellises that supported the jasmine: now they're back up, and clean. They were hanging together by a thread, so we fixed that, and now they're on the correct side of the terrace. You'll find the jasmine a little bare, but it's just so it can come back stronger. By that point, we'd cleared the satellite dish, but we didn't know how to take it apart, since it needed unscrewing. The more we worked, the more jasmine appeared. We've added plumbago, mermaid roses and cross vines. Do you remember that piece of wood that was rotting away behind the railing? We've retrieved that, cut out the rotting bits (some pieces of bamboo fence that were too far gone) and found a decent piece of trellis underneath it all, which we've used to hold up the second jasmine bush. We've rearranged the bay laurel, the laurel and the honeysuckle bush in a wall beneath the roses. I don't have pictures because as soon as we finished, the thunderstorm that had been brewing all day finally broke. That's a good thing, at any rate: rain is a real godsend after repotting. We've scraped under the pots. We've acidified the soil by adding extra peat. We've moved the golden privet. And planted an Asiatic jasmine to cover your window instead. We've moved the rhododendron, the azalea and the laurels downstairs. Back upstairs, we've filled a large box with new herbs (methyst Bowles's mauve, festuca methystine, ballota and stipe) and with the rose that Nico's babysitter gave you as a gift. We've added an eupathorium to the jasmine pot, and a petrorhagia next to the strawberry tree. Oh, and we got rid of a broken watering pipe that ran down the left side – I'm taking it to the skip tomorrow.

All in all, we filled six sacks and several buckets with war debris. To think that the osmanthus was the only plant that needed urgent care! That's why I'm a little wiped out. The only thing I need to explain to you when we meet is that, when you're doing a clean-up like this, any structural flaws become more obvious: there's a crack in the chimney, for instance, and seepage through the roof, as well as a bunch of other little annoyances you should be aware of, like antenna cables dangling here and there, and a watering pipe that leaks out in the garden (we only spotted it when we looked down, after removing the plants). Anyway, aside from that, we were satisfied and happy with our work. Everything's looking tidier and cleaner, ready for the new season. We've locked up the house, checking twice. Apologies for such a long list, but I wanted to keep you properly in the loop. You'll see it all when you're back, and then we can put the finishing touches together. Pino will send you an invoice in the morning. And I will too. Kisses, Maria

If we've all been repotted, if we've all found a new place to be, and if we're all seeds — like the ones Nico planted last year — this is the time of year for us all to bloom. I am lucky to have found myself in a new place, full of sunlight. I will grow very tall, very yellow. I will produce seeds for the blackbirds. How many people can say that they know how to make seeds for the blackbirds?

I'm on my way back from England, but flights keep getting cancelled because of a storm called Gea. It seems like a bad omen. Between London and Milan there are high winds, hail and giant clouds, yet my flight is confirmed.

I sit down on the plane. I speak to the pilot. He reassures me, but then he says, 'We can't leave for another hour, because they've shut everything down in France.'

I ask him if I should get off the plane and explain, very sincerely, that I'd rather not die. He tells me not to get off the plane. I won't die today, but as for tomorrow, he cannot tell. He can't guarantee that. I sit back in my seat.

'I could die in a storm called Gea,' I say to my mother on the phone.

'It's called Gea: you won't die,' my mother says.

'That's one hell of an ending for my book. But you'd have to write it instead.'

'OK,' my mother says, munching on something. I can tell she's distracted. We take off. The plane flies steadily through lightning. We land, and, as it turns out, I'm still alive.

We're organising a birthday party for me, at my mother's place. My grandmother's there, along with my sister Diana, my brother, his wife, little Gea who isn't a storm and Nico. My beautiful boyfriend is there. We bring out the ping-pong table that, at least here, we're allowed to have. We light up tea candles, pour vodka and wine into glasses. Nico gets us all to dance, playing music for us on an old 1960s record player. Mr Bharat is staying at my mother's and joins in with the celebrations when he gets back from his working day, looking for old printing machines to bring back to life. He really likes the food at our house and eats lots of it. In our house we like it when someone eats lots of what we make. Mr Bharat shows us the fake nails he produces in one of his Indian factories, sticking them onto our fingers. He explains how to do it at least one thousand seven hundred times, but we keep listening to him as if he were teaching us a revolutionary mantra. Peel it, stick it, press it. It must be his Indian voice and Indian smile. Even my father comes. My father and Mr Bharat play ping-pong together, while my mother dances a twist with Nico. My father and Mr Bharat converse in an absurd variety of English, made of few words, heavy accents and long, eternal pauses. I can tell that my father is dying to win the match. He's laughing, but he definitely wants to win. When he misses a ball, he lets out a strange noise and says, 'Nice one, goddamn'. Later, as he's playing against my son, he says the same thing: 'Nice one, goddamn'. Everyone takes turns challenging everyone else. I drink to my heart's content, and I am happy, because my mother is dancing the twist. I'm also happy because my father continues to eat.

They sing Happy Birthday, and I blow out my candles.

'Make a wish,' they scream.

I'm always afraid they'll forget to ask, and I won't have a chance to make my wish. But they're all smiling, looking expectantly at me. I look back at them, one by one, then I smile as well. We're all different heights, with different noses and eyes, different beginnings, different endings. I feel an unquantifiable amount of love, and an unquantifiable amount of distance: we will never end, I've never been here, here I am. I wasn't the first at any one thing and not one thing ends with me. I make the same wish I always make – one I cannot reveal but that, luckily, keeps coming true. Is it luck? I put all my effort into blowing out my candles. So I think, actually, maybe I'm just doing an excellent job.

'Many happy returns,' says Mr Bharat. I've never heard this sentence before, which is used for birthdays in India. 'Come back happily again.' Incarnate many other times in your future lives, happily. I'm thinking it's a better way to put it than simply saying 'happy birthday' to someone, especially in the middle of all this movement.

My boyfriend, Nico and I spend the night at my mother's.

'Many happy returns,' we keep saying to one another.

'Who's my favourite person on Earth? My greatest, most absolute love?' I ask Nico.

'Yourself,' he answers, immediately. For a moment, I feel both like laughing and crying.

'And who's your favourite person on Earth, your everlasting love forever?' I ask him, after a beat.

'Myself!' he says. So I can start breathing again.

When I wake up, the psychic is making curry. It's dark outside. Her wallpaper is covered in avocado leaves. There are parrots, even a zebra.

'Everything OK?' she asks. I nod. I am lying next to a new pink quartz, three times my size. 'You need to stay still,' the psychic says.

'I can't: I want everyone. I want to go everywhere. See everything.'

'You'll have a baby girl. You'll grow older. Your son will marry as a young man. This book will exist. That's whether you want it or not, whether or not you're in movement.'

I count to a hundred. Then up to two hundred. I breathe

in the way I've been taught in my yoga classes. I blink my eyes quickly.

'Are you done making a scene?' the psychic asks me.

I stop blinking and trying to wake myself from a dream. I run my hand on the table and smell its wood.

'If I were you, I'd eat my curry. I run an Indian food delivery service in the evenings.'

'Are you Indian?' I ask.

'Jamaican,' the psychic says.

I help her set the table and she serves me vegetable curry, rice and bancha tea. A bunch of flowers have appeared in the sink. I arrange them in a vase.

'Are you eating?' I ask.

'I'm watching you,' the psychic says, as she watches me eat the best curry I've ever had in my life. I chew the food, and once I feel full, I clear the table, washing my own bowl and cutlery. Since the psychic isn't saying a thing, I copy her movements, as we wrap up a dozen portions of curry and a dozen portions of rice. We put our coats on, switch off the lights and leave her flat. It's freezing outside.

'Get on,' she says, pointing at an orange moped.

'Brrr,' I whisper.

'Yoo-hoo!' she screams.

I sit behind the psychic, and for a couple of hours we deliver curries, mapping out the city of London through our movement. My eyes fill up with tears. When it isn't too windy, I throw my head back and watch street lamps, tunnel lighting, office neon stream above me. At midnight, I realise we're outside my boyfriend's door. My own door, perhaps.

'Ah,' I say. 'We're home.'

The psychic hugs me tight. I let her hug me.

'Hug me back!' she smiles.

So I hug her back.

'Thank you,' I say. Then I add: 'How much for the tarot reading, the curry and everything else?'

'Hmmm, five by five. Six minus one. How much's that?' She counts on her fingers, then explodes into laughter. 'A billion pounds! Do you have that?'

I shake my head.

'All right, I'll take ten thousand billion and that's my final offer. You can pay me next time. I don't expect you have that amount in your pocket,' she says. 'Or do you?'

I look in my pockets. Maybe I have something. I shake my head.

'Look better,' she laughs.

I rummage again and a sliver of something cuts my finger.

'Ouch,' I say.

I raise my finger to take a better look and see that a piece of pink quartz has slipped under my skin, splitting my digit. I put the finger in my mouth, swallowing the quartz fragment. When I look up again, the psychic is no longer there, and my fingerprint is forever altered.

Before I Disappear

I'm home with Nico. We're drawing invitation cards for a party he wants to hold by the crooked tree in the park. Earlier today he cried because some of his classmates told him they didn't feel like coming to his party. He stuck his fingers into the corners of his eyes to block the tears, so I couldn't tell he was crying. I stick my fingers into my eyes too. He doesn't want to show me that he is crying, and I don't want to show him I'm crying. I suggest to Nico we hold a vegetable workshop on the terrace instead of a party by the crooked tree. We could invite thirty other kids, or maybe three billion, however many he wants to invite – I'm game. He pretends not to hear me. Maybe I didn't actually say it.

My sister Diana calls me. 'Are you free to talk?' she says on the phone. 'I wanted to tell you something.'

'Go for it.'

'I was cycling last night when I saw two motorbikes on the ground next to an ambulance. They looked like

Alessandro's and his best friend Tommaso's. So I called Alessandro.'

I pull Nico onto my lap. He wants to be in my lap and won't continue to draw if I'm not drawing too.

'His mobile rang, and then he picked up. How are you, I said. I'm well, thanks, he said. Thank God for that, I said. I'm in Via Eustachi and there's a motorbike down that looks exactly like yours, and another that looks exactly like Tommaso's. There was a pause on the line. And then Alessandro said: 'I'm in the ambulance. The motorbike's mine.'

'How is he? How are they?' I ask.

I'm scared. Nico kisses me and starts drawing again. Now he wants to draw, even though I'm not drawing.

'I get into the ambulance and Alessandro tells me: call your sister! He wanted me to let you know, for your book, you see,' she laughs. 'They had a bit of a scare, but they're OK. It was the other person's fault – a lady jumped a red light. Alessandro said that he was thinking of his son as he flew off his bike.'

'Where are they now?'

'In the hospital. The same one. In the ambulance we had a bit of a scene: they asked me if I was his wife and whether Alessandro wanted me there. In the end he had to explain that it wasn't that he didn't want me there, but there was someone else now – I wasn't his girlfriend anymore. It was still us, though it was no longer us like before.'

When I hang up, I write to Alessandro: 'I didn't need the kind of denouement that involves a car accident. Thanks for your help, but now, please go back to your son and smash that old bike of yours into pieces. Take it slowly. I hug you, Anna.'

That night, Nico and I slip into the same bed. He's become tall. He talks in his sleep and keeps me awake. I grab my phone and call my ex-husband. He picks up on the second ring. I tell him that today Nico was sad, because of his friends.

'Don't worry. Kids will be kids. They always will be. Nico is very sensitive. He has a sensitive mum, a sensitive dad and now you have a new sensitive boyfriend, and I have a new sensitive girlfriend. His grandparents are sensitive. He's surrounded by sensitive people,' my ex-husband says. 'Poor boy, that's a whole bunch of sensitivity to deal with.'

'Isn't that a good thing?' I ask.

'Getting angry is a good thing too, sometimes. Anyway, you should ring me whenever you're feeling concerned.'

If I'm concerned, I'm allowed to ring him again. We're now at a distance that allows for it. The following morning, I ring Maria to tell her about the accident.

'Tell me while I'm tending to the plants,' she says, 'so it's like I'm giving myself horticultural therapy.'

I listen as she opens the door and goes into the garden. I hear the birds sing, the wind. I imagine Maria's stumpy tortoise crawling forward next to her. Go, tortoise!

'You won't be connected forever,' I say, to allow the elephant in the room to take part in our conversation. The Roland Ultra peeps in, still convinced it is an animal. 'It's not like something will happen to you now, just because Alessandro had another accident. Let's go back to the beginning of this scene, actually. Alessandro falls, but he doesn't break. I tell you calmly, without too many adjectives. You listen to me, and nothing bad happens.'

'Last time I got sick twelve hours after his accident. How long has it been?' she asks. Her voice sounds scared, but she wants to keep calm, I can tell. Alessandro is OK. She's OK. They're not connected. Or maybe they are connected, but not in a dramatic, fatal way that means if one of them gets hurt, then the other also will. Swarms. Irrigation systems. Forest.

'It's already been over fifteen hours,' I tell her.

'Maybe it'd been fifteen hours last time, and I don't remember it correctly.'

We talk about other things: her dishwasher, her boyfriend. Deliberately, with purpose, we take our minds elsewhere. A few minutes later, Alessandro texts: I'm incredibly well. Unscathed. I've even spent the night in A&E next to a porn star.

Summer's back again and Nico has almost finished nursery. After the holidays, he'll start primary school. He wishes there was no money in the world so there wouldn't be wars. He writes a six-minute song on the topic and asks me to send it to the mayor of Milan. Two weeks pass and every day Nico asks whether the mayor of Milan replied. I explain to him that the mayor is a very busy man, and that he probably won't get back to him, but that isn't because he doesn't care. He just doesn't have the time. So it is with great surprise that, by the end of the fifteenth day, I open my email account and see that the mayor of Milan has replied. Nico is happy about the letter in the same way as he's happy when I send him a postcard from a place far away, or when he receives a fake letter from Santa Claus. When people are far apart, they write I love you to each other. Seeds make sunflowers that make other seeds.

Nico and I have plenty of flowers. Plenty of figs that I eat every day but Nico won't even taste. There are so many lemons there's no chance they'll all ripen: the tree can't withstand such a bounty of fruit. The echinacea grows strong; the lavender is tall and deliciously perfumed. The ivy is spreading to cover the walls, and in time it will produce other cracks. Nico makes lemonade with our lemons and there are seventeen different varieties of tomatoes growing in our crates.

'Many people think that a plant bearing lots of fruit is an indication of its health,' Maria explains. 'You don't know how often I hear the same thing: but it was doing so well! It was full of flowers, full of fruit, how come it died?'

'I already know I will like what you are about to say,' I tell her.

'Plants need to survive, and their last chance at this is to put out as many children as possible into the world. They squeeze out all they can, before they disappear. So sometimes, an explosion of flowers or fruit precedes a plant's death.'

During this time, the newspapers are full of photographs about the jellyfish emergency. The sea is pink, full of jelly heads and stinging tentacles. Nico and I decide we should seriously start to breed turtles, so we can repopulate the sea with them. The turtles will eat the jellyfish and then we'll be able to float on our backs on the surface of the water again. We could become turtle breeders, run gardening workshops for children and eliminate all money from planet Earth. All mayors will say yes to us through the medium of email.

'Why does time pass so fast?' Nico often asks.

'I don't know,' I always reply.

'Why don't you know that?'

'I don't know because I don't know.'

When he's out in the world, Nico is often crouching, as kids do, and I look at the place where he is crouching. Only twenty centimetres separate him from the floor, ants, breadcrumbs, hair and debris, and I wouldn't even notice these things if he weren't crouching there, illuminating them all with his gaze, touching them with his fingers. Touch as many things as you can! Stay! Put out more fruit before you disappear.

'I will miss you,' Nico tells me now, when I'm about to leave.

'I will miss you too,' I say.

'Will you cry?' he asks.

'Maybe.'

'I will.'

If we're leaving together, he holds onto my hand. He walks steadily and when we arrive on the island, it is just the two of us, Nico and me. We enjoy that now. My boyfriend will join us later, and that's how we like it. For the first few days, we remain on land, sitting on the sand or on the rocky bank, looking at the water only from a distance. Eventually, we make up our minds, and hire a paddle boat. From this new beach, safe upon the water surface, we survey things. Some bays and coves have been completely overtaken by jellyfish. The jellyfish float. They're in movement. They fluctuate, and they scare us. They bump into each other, taking over the whole galaxy, turning the whole planet fluorescent. I look around me and I can't see a single human being. We paddle again towards the coast, without being able to swim. We sit on the sand with our chins on our knees. We need to come up with something.

'Are you writing?' my mother asks on the phone.

She's on loudspeaker as I'm driving back home. The salt mountains are already behind us.

'All the time!' Nico replies from the back seat.

We all laugh and switch the subject to what books we are reading and how much Nico's eating. The games he wants for his birthday and how cold it is today, and how hot it is today. It is both hot and cold, as it always is in this month, but also, it is hot and it is cold as it is hot and cold uniquely and exactly today, and for us only, in our particular spot of the universe, in the square centimetres we occupy and on our skin.

The following morning, Nico and I buy two fishing nets.

'My life dream is catching jellyfish,' he says.

'I didn't know that.'

'Me neither.'

A little before the sun sets, as the light reflects off the top of the jellyfish, we take out the paddle boat again. It's a funny boat, shaped like a red car, with a slide in the middle of it. It looks a bit like a miniature version of the Roland Ultra. Nico picked it because it's red, and because it's a car with a slide on top of it. I would have preferred the blue paddle boat, with no car and no slide. Pedalling alone hurts my thighs. Nico is resting his feet on the pedals, but his legs are too short to help me. How will I help him when I have no strength left? Will I manage to keep him from dying? Will he manage to keep me from dying? We pedal on, the sea rushing quickly under our boat, as we pick the most infested bay of all. A sea of pink lives under the blue sea. We try to hold all the love on planet Earth in our bodies, while the Earth becomes more and more distant. I tie the paddle boat to a rock shaped like a heart. We, too, will have marked our passage on Earth for a short time. On the boat, we lie on our bellies and direct our eyes towards the bottom of the sea. The sun warms our shoulders and the nape of our necks as we lie still for a moment, observing the wonders of the depths. Then we sit up and start fishing for jellyfish.

'I'm expecting a baby girl,' I say.

'Where are you expecting her?' he asks.

'Wherever you are.'

Nico is happy. A rocket flashes over our heads. Then a silver airship. Soon, a spaceship joins them.

'Thank you,' I say to Nico, pointing up at the sky.

He looks at me, smiles and goes back to his fishing.

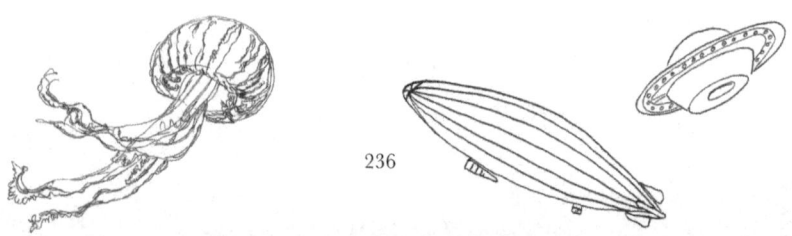

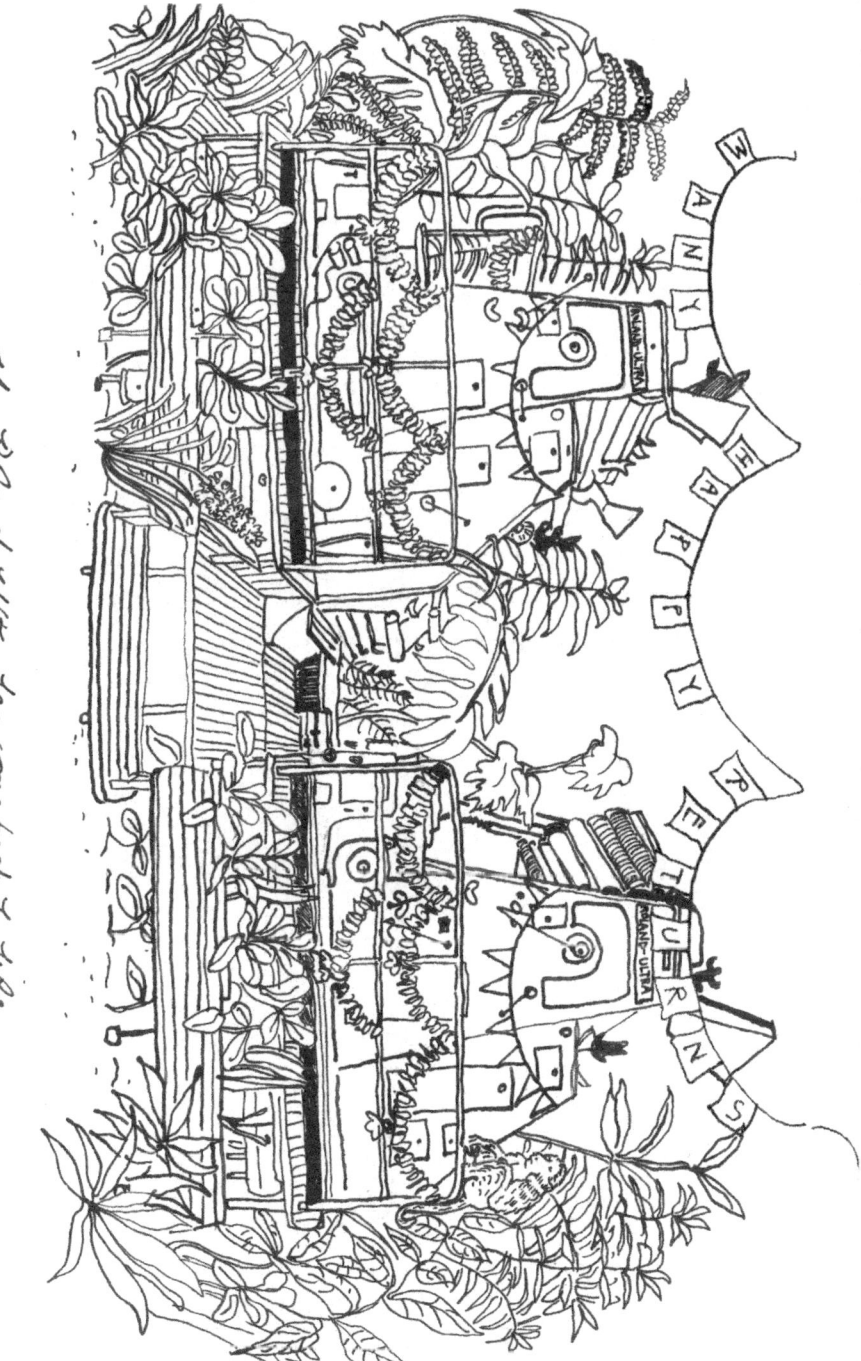

The Roland ULlia has come back to life

About the author

Ilaria Bernardini is a writer, screenwriter and TV show creator. She is the author of nine novels, translated in various countries, two graphic novels and two collections of short stories. Her book *The Girls Are Good* was recently adapted into a six-part TV series for Paramount+.